Bones Gather No Moss

John Sherwood

CHARLES SCRIBNER'S SONS

New York London Toronto Sydney Tokyo Singapore

CHARLES SCRIBNER'S SONS
Rockefeller Center
1230 Avenue of the Americas
New York, NY 10020

First published in Great Britain by Macmillan London Limited

SCRIBNERS and colophon are registered
trademarks of Macmillan, Inc.

Manufactured in the United States of America

ISBN: 0-684-19738-3

ONE

Sir Hugo Mackenzie stood at the entrance of Saint Margaret's church, Westminster, as crowds of the great and good filed past him to attend the memorial service for a friend and colleague. Geoffrey Maitland had ended his career as British ambassador in Paris, then died at a ripe old age. Sir Hugo's own age was even riper, and the way the ranks were thinning out disquieted him a little. But what really worried him was that the memorial service had also become a date with Adrienne de Fleury.

He had not seen Adrienne for at least twelve years. And it was almost forty since they had been, for a brief period, lovers. Her telephone call from France had come out of the blue. Was he proposing to attend Geoffrey Maitland's memorial service? she wondered. He was? Perfect. She wanted to see him, so if she came over, would he be very *gentil* and give her lunch afterwards? He agreed, but was uneasy. Why was she crossing the English Channel to attend the memorial service of a man who had not been a personal friend? She was a very devious woman, who seldom did anything without an ulterior end in view. She had come because she wanted to see him. But why?

Adrienne's late husband, Edouard de Fleury de Marcilly, had been a senior French diplomat. Edouard and Adrienne had been close friends of Sir Hugo's, for at several stages in their diplomatic careers their postings in foreign capitals had coincided. The love affair had occurred in Bucharest, partly because Hugo, as a youngish

1

widower, was fair game, and partly because social life in a Cold War East European capital was boringly restricted and there was nothing much else to do. Later, in Lagos, and later still in Buenos Aires, he had had to resist determined and cunning campaigns by Adrienne to interest him in various women with a view to a second marriage. As he stood waiting for her outside the church, wondering what she wanted from him, he reflected that she was quite capable of having evolved an embarrassing plan to marry him off to herself.

She had never been punctual in her habits and he resigned himself to a long wait. Former colleagues, often looking alarmingly old, went past him into the church. Then suddenly there she was, descending from her taxi, a tall, imposing figure in ageless, understated clothes, with the unmistakable air of a great lady. She had stopped dyeing her hair, it was white under the scrap of church-going black lace on her head. But her eyes were still startlingly blue. Age had been kind to her on the whole.

'Ah, 'Ugo, *mon chéri*! What a joy to see you again!'

As in duty bound he kissed her on both cheeks, then on the right one again, slightly embarrassed by the attention their embrace was getting from a former Permanent Secretary on his way into the church. When their faces were far enough apart to make scrutiny possible, he saw a network of fine wrinkles. But hers was the kind of beauty which survives the ravages of time.

'You have hardly changed at all,' he murmured as they took their places inside.

'*Chéri*, I adore you when you tell unconvincing lies,' she whispered, and laid her hand affectionately on his arm. He became even more anxious and puzzled. Clearly she wanted something. Whatever it was would probably disrupt his quiet, ordered life in a Sussex village, and he hated any threat to his settled habits.

The service began. As it ran its course, he wondered how Adrienne had found out that it was taking place. Had she subscribed to the airmail edition of *The Times*

2

and scanned the court page till she found a suitable pretext for coming to London and making a date with him? It was only a pretext, he was sure of that. He had worked it out that she and Edouard had been *en poste* in Pretoria throughout Geoffrey Maitland's tenure of the Paris embassy. Could they have met earlier, in some posting elsewhere? Perhaps, but with what result? Even as a junior attaché Maitland had been a cautious young man, with no appetite for romps in the hay with married women.

Someone embarked on a eulogy, with particular emphasis on the late lamented's brilliant conduct of Britain's relations with France during a particularly difficult period. During the closing hymn, Sir Hugo reflected that relations with France were never anything but difficult; and that Maitland's stint in Paris would have been even more brilliant if he had not been encumbered with a wife with no dress sense who spoke French with an accent which only the British could understand.

In the taxi on the way to lunch at his club, he put the question direct. 'Adrienne, how did you find out about the memorial service?'

'Oh, it was simple, *mon cher* 'Ugo. When poor Maitland died there was a necrological notice in *Le Figaro*. I knew there would be a memorial service, so I asked your embassy in Paris to tell me when it would be.'

'How well did you know him?'

'Not at all.' She gave his arm a warm squeeze. 'It was only an excuse to come and see you.'

Sir Hugo became even more alarmed. To create a diversion, he began asking for news of old friends they had in common. Nothing further of an untoward nature occurred during the taxi ride, and by the time he had settled her down at a lunch table in his club, the Travellers, he thought it wise to enquire into her personal circumstances, which might provide a clue to whatever devious scheme she was trying to involve him in.

It turned out that after Edouard's death she had gone

3

on living in the family château, which was in the country south-west of Orleans. Chantal, her daughter, and Jean-Louis, her son, were both married, and were living there too.

'I suppose they inherited Fleury when Edouard died,' said Sir Hugo.

'Of course.' She made a serio-comic grimace. 'Edouard naturally left the house to them *en indivision*.'

Horrors, Sir Hugo thought. Under French law, a testator was obliged to leave his house to all his children as their joint property. There were various arrangements under which this could be done, but to leave it *en indivision* was a sure-fire recipe for a bitter family quarrel, because the house could not be sold unless all the beneficiaries agreed to do so. When the family reunion met to decide what should be done, some would be in favour of selling it and dividing the proceeds. No, one of them would insist, it was our home, it is full of our memories. To sell it to strangers would be heartbreaking, how could anyone suggest such a barbarity? A firm objection from one of the parties made a sale legally impossible. But if it was not sold, who was to pay for maintaining it? Which of them was to live in it? If one of them could buy the others out and move in, the problem was solved. But the family money had often been left in such a way that none of them could afford that, and the empty house would fall further and further into decay while an internecine family quarrel about what to do with it rumbled on into the next generation.

There was probably no question of selling the Château de Fleury, which had been in the family for centuries. It was quite large enough for Jean-Louis and Chantal to instal themselves in separate bits of it with their families. But any divided inheritance left plenty of room for disagreement, and from what Sir Hugo remembered of the Fleury children, he did not trust them to deal with the problems in a civilized manner. He remembered Chantal as a teenager who insisted on having her own way, and

4

Jean-Louis as an intriguer who was already showing promise as an unscrupulous sex-athlete. Even as children, they had quarrelled.

'Do they fight?' he asked.

She gave him a quick little smile. 'No, not really, they are nice children, very good to me.'

In view of what he remembered about Jean-Louis and Chantal, he reverted to a piece of tradecraft he had learnt from past dealings with Adrienne. To find out whether she was lying, one watched her hands, not her face. Sure enough, they had gone tense.

'Are they good to each other? They used not to be.'

'You are right, cats and dogs were honey by comparison. But it's better now.'

Was it? The smile had become fixed and her hands were so tense that her knife and fork were trembling a little. She was obviously planning something. Perhaps the idea was to get him over to Fleury and make him mediate between the warring factions. The prospect of having to go to France and bang disagreeable middle-aged heads together appalled him. Searching for safer conversational ground, he remembered that Jean-Louis was not the only son. There had been another one, a rather beautiful little boy with a tendency to keep smelly pet animals. With an effort, memory even produced a name.

'And . . . Paul-Henri? He is not living with you?'

Suddenly her face was tragic. 'He is not living at all. He died eleven years ago, in an accident with his car.'

'Oh my dear, I am sorry.'

She was so upset that she had put down her fork, unable to eat. 'Poor Paul-Henri, he was such a dear boy, not at all practical like the others but always up in the clouds. But clever, he had more grey substance in his head than Jean-Louis and Chantal together. He had excellent results in his studies, and he always knew what he wanted to do. He was obsessed, you see, with nature, you remember all those animals he kept as a child? He had turned from animals to plants, he had set himself the enormous

5

task of recording all the savage flowers of France.'

'The wild flowers? How admirable.'

'Yes, before they were destroyed by pesticides and industrial development. He had won grants from various foundations, and he went around all the regions of France making careful scientific drawings of them. He had an old van that he had found somewhere, and he spent his summers living in this van while he collected his specimens and made his drawings. In the winter he was at Fleury consulting his botanical books and organizing his collection.'

She wiped her eyes, and began toying with her fork again. 'All his drawings, hundreds of them, are still in the library at Fleury. Perhaps you remember that he had a certain artistic talent. Experts who have seen them pronounce them truly remarkable. Everyone agrees that they should be published.'

He nodded. 'As a fitting memorial for poor Paul-Henri.'

'I have a favour to ask of you, *mon cher*. No, don't look so stricken by panic, I'm not planning to take you into my bed again. You can help me, please, to approach the competent authorities.'

Alarmed, he protested that nowadays he was an old fogey with no influence in high places, but she swept on. 'It is connected with this affair of poor Paul-Henri. I am looking for an editor to arrange his drawings in the proper classifications and prepare them for publication in a book.'

'What a splendid idea. But I'm afraid I know nothing whatever about who's who in French botanical circles.'

She waved her fork at him dismissively. 'I am looking for an English editor, not a Frenchman.'

'But surely, Adrienne, the book would have to be published in French? The editor would have to be French, someone who knows the popular names of the French wild flowers and that sort of thing.'

'No. If the editor arranges the drawings according to the proper classifications, with the Latin names attached, everything else can be added later.'

'But in that sort of book the plants have to be

6

described, surely, in special botanical terms. The shape of the leaves, the parts of the flower, and so on.'

'All that can be written in English, and translated.'

'Who by?'

'By me. You forget that Edouard spent half his diplomatic career in English-speaking countries.'

'But botanical jargon can scarcely be described as English. Few English people understand it.'

'With a good dictionary, I shall manage.'

'Surely there must be someone in France who could do the job?'

'No. In France hardly anyone takes a serious interest in botany, and among the few who do there is bitter jealousy and competition. The only people qualified whom I found were preparing similar editions of their own.'

There was something very odd about this. Did France really contain no suitably qualified botanist? If no one French could be found, what about French-speaking Switzerland?

Under his questioning gaze, Adrienne avoided his eye. 'The botanical culture is much better developed here than in France.'

While she was talking, Sir Hugo had reached one firm conclusion. He knew one person who was fully qualified for the job, his niece Celia Grant. She had been taught French very thoroughly by a brutal governess, and had spent two miserable terms at a Swiss finishing school before she persuaded her parents to let her go to Wye Agricultural College instead and take a degree in horticulture. But he was determined not to let Celia's name pass his lips. He did not believe for a moment in the memorial volume. There was no reason why it could not be edited in France, and anyway, why had Adrienne waited eleven years before embarking on the project? She was up to some mischief, and he did not intend to involve Celia in it.

'You had a niece, I remember, who was studying botany,' said Adrienne casually.

So that was it. She had remembered that somehow, and

had mounted this whole elaborate ploy as a scheme to get her hooks into Celia through him.

'My niece Celia Grant is a very busy career woman,' he said firmly. 'She has a large horticultural business to run, and I'm sure she wouldn't consider your proposal.'

'You're sure? She has other cats to whip?'

'What you mean is, she has other fish to fry. No decent person in Britain would dream of whipping a cat.'

'That's true, you prefer to whip each other. About animals you are ridiculously sentimental.'

The conversation had come to a full stop. He saw now what Adrienne was up to. She must have heard in some roundabout way that Celia sometimes operated as a private detective. The fable about Paul-Henri's botanical drawings was a pretext, to get her to Fleury and sort out some frightful family situation there. Well, there was nothing doing.

'If your niece cannot undertake the work herself,' said Adrienne, 'perhaps she can recommend me to someone suitable. She must have connections among such people, she will perhaps know of a qualified person. Please, 'Ugo *chéri*, be kind and ask her to suggest some names.'

He decided to do nothing of the kind. There was no point in getting Celia to 'suggest names'. Adrienne had only asked for some to disguise the fact that Celia herself was the only 'botanist' she wanted.

But she kept up the pretence to the last. As he saw her into her taxi she turned. 'Please, *mon cher* 'Ugo, do not forget to ask your niece for some names. I shall be back at Fleury tomorrow evening, you can telephone me there with the answer.'

He expected to hear no more. But two days later Adrienne rang him from France. 'You have spoken to your niece, 'Ugo?'

'I'm sorry, no. I've been rather busy.'

'Do please speak to her as soon as you can, and ask her for the names. I rely on you.'

Curiouser and curiouser. His suspicions were obviously

wrong, and he saw now that they were rather far-fetched. How could Adrienne possibly have known about Celia's disastrous inability to resist the lure of curiosity? And if she did know, how did she also know that Celia had good enough French to operate effectively at Fleury? Far from wanting Celia to go there and detect, she genuinely wanted a qualified botanist from England to work on Paul-Henri's drawings.

But why did she insist on someone English? When he put the situation to Celia on the phone, she confirmed that it would not have been difficult to find a qualified Frenchman.

'No, perfectly easy, I should think. The great pundit is a man called Gaston Bonnier at the Sorbonne. He's a bit too grand, but I'm sure he could suggest somebody with the right qualifications. Why does she want someone from here?'

'Goodness knows. She really wanted you, that's why she approached me. I said no on your behalf, I hope I did right.'

'Horrors, yes. Thank you.'

'And now she wants you to suggest some names.'

'But Uncle Hugo, the whole carry-on sounds mad to me. Botanical classifications are supposed to be international, but there are minor variations in taxonomy from country to country, and no one here would know what the French botanists have changed their minds about lately. Besides, who here knows enough French to write the introduction and botanical descriptions?'

'It's to be written in English, she says, and she'll translate it.'

'Horrors. D'you think she knows the French for a ciliate epicalyx or a papillose involucre?'

'No, but I've got to get her off my back somehow.'

'Why don't you tell her I can't think of anyone suitable, but I'm sure she'll find someone French if she tries hard enough.'

'I will if you really can't think of anyone.'

9

While he was nerving himself to ring Adrienne with this stern message, Celia spoke again. 'Hold on a moment, I think I've had an idea.'

'Ah. Good.'

'How well paid is this job, Uncle Hugo?'

'Lavishly, she says.'

'Then ... I think I know someone who might jump at it. A woman called Jane Greenwood, who's just been made redundant by her university. Her lecturership's been abolished, and she has an elderly mother to support.'

'Tell me about her. Does she have fluent French?'

'I shouldn't think so, but does that matter?'

'I suppose not, but would it be right for me to project an innocent wild-flower lady into what I suspect is a château full of bitter family hatreds?'

'If the bitter family hatreds take place in French, she won't notice.'

'Perhaps, but I distrust this whole set-up. Adrienne's very devious, you should have seen some of the women she tried to marry me off to after your aunt died. Why does she want an English editor unless she's up to something?'

'You may be right, but on the other hand, Jane Greenwood's desperate for money.'

'Could she do the job?'

'Oh yes. She's an expert on something obscure and boring, mosses and liverworts I think. But she's fully qualified to do a general wild-flower job, if that's what's wanted. Look, she lives quite near you, somewhere the other side of Lewes. Why don't you go and have a talk with her, then decide whether to throw her to the lions?'

'Very well, if you think she'd do.'

Next day Sir Hugo went to interview Dr Greenwood. She was in her fifties, tall, fair haired and rather handsome. She struck him as level headed, competent, and likely to keep her head in a crisis. As she made no secret of the fact that she needed well-paid employment urgently, he persuaded himself that there would be no crisis, and passed on her name and address to Adrienne.

Cross-channel negotiations followed on the telephone and by letter. A fortnight later, Dr Jane Greenwood, B.Sc., Ph.D., loaded all her reference books, her portable typewriter and her microscope into her elderly Mini, stocked up the freezer with food for her mother and drove down to Dover, to launch herself across the English Channel into the unknown.

A month later, on a hot afternoon in June, a milling crowd of gardening enthusiasts was poring over the plants in the frame yard at Archerscroft Nurseries, many of them rarities unobtainable elsewhere. Business was brisk. But as usual some of the shoppers were more enthusiastic than knowledgeable. In particular, those with chalky soil seemed to be fatally attracted to calcifuge plants which would die on them within weeks, so that Celia Grant and Bill Wilkins, her head gardener, were kept busy persuading them to switch to substitutes. Halfway through the afternoon Mary Basset, who had been detailed to look out for shoplifters, paraded before Celia a tall man with a military air whom she had caught trying to make off with a *Mimulus glutinosus* secreted in a carrier bag. In dealing with him Celia became very icy and ladylike, because she knew that she was only five feet three inches tall and slim, with silver-grey hair, and that if she raised her voice and behaved angrily she would look and sound like the Queen of the Fairies in a tantrum. Having told the offender coldly never to darken the gates of Archerscroft Nurseries again, she hurried off to inform an eager young couple that *Iris stylosa* 'Mary Barnard' would hate being planted in the damp margin of their lily pool.

There was still an hour to go before closing time when one of the girls manning the cash register approached her with unwelcome news. 'There's someone to see you, Mrs Grant. In your office. A policeman.'

Celia cursed inwardly. What could he want? Nothing to do with shoplifting, surely? It was her policy to deal with that without involving the police.

He was a young constable from the station in Welstead,

and he did not have shoplifters on his mind. 'Good afternoon, madam. I'm sorry to bother you on a busy afternoon, but it's about Dr Greenwood.'

Dr Greenwood. The moss specialist she had recommended to Uncle Hugo. 'Oh dear, what about her?'

'I understand she's in France.'

'Yes, I believe she is. Why?'

'We've had a call from Lewes police. Her mother has been taken to hospital with a stroke, a very bad one, they say. They want Dr Greenwood to come back home as soon as possible.'

'I'm sorry to hear that, but why have you come to me?'

'We hoped you would have Dr Greenwood's address in France.'

'I'm afraid not. Sir Hugo Mackenzie has it, though. He put her in touch with the people she was going to work for there.'

'So our colleagues in Lewes understood from a friend of the old lady's, the woman who found her.'

'Well, then . . . ?'

'Sir Hugo's away. His housekeeper says he's on holiday abroad, and she doesn't know where to get hold of him.'

Damn Uncle Hugo, Celia thought. 'Isn't there a note of the address somewhere in the Greenwoods' house? Why didn't they go there and look?'

'Sir Hugo's housekeeper felt sure you would have it.'

'Well, I haven't.'

There was a pregnant pause.

'When my gran had a stroke,' the constable remarked, 'the hospital said the important thing was to get a close relative to the bedside as soon as possible, it makes them less afraid and confused.'

'Well, that sounds very sensible to me.'

Another pause followed before he spoke again. 'You see, madam, this isn't strictly speaking a police matter. When things like this happen, and there's no crime involved, we're prepared to alert the relatives and other people concerned, but after that it's up to them.'

'So what you're saying is, you want me to go over to the Greenwoods' house and ransack it for the address?'

'Well yes, madam, if you don't mind.'

He was within his rights, of course. The police had plenty to do without acting as agony aunts to the general public. This situation was Uncle Hugo's responsibility, and if he was out of reach it was up to her to stand in for him. She was dog tired after her long day's work at the nursery, and tried to close her ears to the voice of conscience. But it was no good. One could not leave a frightened old woman with a stroke, in hospital and surrounded by strangers, without trying to do something about it. Instead of having a hot bath and putting her feet up, she would have to drive down to Sussex, find out where in France Dr Greenwood was and phone her with the news about her mother.

'Oh very well,' she said grumpily, and pushed the telephone across the desk to him. 'Ring Lewes police for me, would you? I need to know how to find the house and how I'm to get in.'

Having received instructions, she ate a hasty snack and drove down to Sussex, cross, tired, and feeling rather dirty. The Greenwoods' cottage was one of a pair. The key had been left with the neighbour in the other one, who produced it but kept it firmly in her hand till she had delivered a long defensive speech about the important preoccupations which had prevented her from noticing for twenty-four hours that Mrs Greenwood, instead of following her normal daily routine, was lying unconscious on her kitchen floor. In the end Celia wrested the key from her, dissuaded her from following and let herself in next door.

The Greenwoods' cottage was pleasantly furnished and tidy, apart from the uncleared remains of a simple meal on the living-room table. Anxious to lose no time looking for what she wanted, Celia made straight for the desk, which to her relief was not locked. To judge from the jumble of hoarded paper inside, it was the old lady's, not her daughter's. After a good deal of searching she found a card in one of the pigeon holes, reading: Jane's address: Château de Fleury, Fleury-la-Forêt, and a five-figure post-code. There was also a telephone number. Celia found the Greenwoods' phone and rang it.

It was answered by a woman who sounded like a servant. When Celia asked to speak to Dr Greenwood, there was a marked pause, followed by: '*De la part de qui, madame, s'il vous plaît?*'

Celia gave her name and explained that she was a friend of Dr Greenwood's mother.

Another pause. There seemed to be some difficulty.

'*Un instant, madame. Ne quittez pas.*'

The 'instant' lasted a long time. Then a new voice came on the line, speaking English. 'Hallo, Adrienne de Fleury speaking. I'm afraid my housekeeper didn't exactly get your name?'

'I'm Celia Grant, Sir Hugo Mackenzie's niece.'

'Oh, dear 'Ugo, I have just called him, but his house-keeper says he is not at home.'

'Yes, he's abroad. I rang to speak to Dr Greenwood. Her mother's been taken very ill. She'll have to come home.'

'Oh. You know, this is very awkward.'

'Is it? Why?'

'Dr Greenwood isn't here.'

'Could you tell me where she can be reached?'

'I can't, unfortunately. It is quite a mystery. She left here in her car the other day, on an excursion connected with the botanical work she is doing for me. We expected to see her again in the evening, but she did not come. I am very anxious concerning her.'

Horrors, Celia thought. Had the woman bolted? Why?

'She took nothing with her,' Madame de Fleury went on. 'No clothes, no *articles de toilette*, not even her pass-port. Everything is still in her room.'

Worse and worse. 'In that case,' Celia argued, 'there must have been some kind of accident.'

14

'I think so, yes.'

'How long is it since she disappeared?'

'Three days. I was away when it happened, but after she had failed to reappear my son informed the gendarmerie. I returned only this afternoon, and tried at once to ring dear 'Ugo with a message.'

'What are the gendarmerie doing about it? It really is very important to find her.'

'In these times of disorder and crime the gendarmerie have many other tasks to perform.' A note of suppressed panic crept into her voice. 'I am old, they keep asking me questions, this affair torments and bewilders me. I was telephoning dear 'Ugo to ask him to come and give me support, because when such things happen one does not know where to point one's head. Can you perhaps come in his place?'

Celia hesitated. 'Aren't your family there? Can't they rally round?'

'No!'

It was a cry of distress. Clearly, she did not count on the family for support. Celia remembered what Sir Hugo had said: the Château de Fleury was a mass of bitter family hatreds.

'Please come,' Adrienne pleaded. 'The police will show themselves more energetic if a representative of the victim's family is there watching them.'

Pity struck Celia as she thought of old Mrs Greenwood lying in hospital, confused and unable to speak, and wondering why her daughter did not come. But along with the pity there was also the rather shocking little stir of excitement which was her normal response to a mystery that needed solving. Moreover it was the time of year when she always got a bit bored with Archerscroft. Nothing very exciting was coming along in the seedbeds or glasshouses, the autumn catalogue had gone off to the printers already and it was not time yet to start planting and sowing again. The flogging of plants to the public could go on perfectly well in her absence. In

15

fact the urge to escape from drudgery was pointing firmly in the same direction as the voice of conscience.

'I think I could slip across for a day or two,' she said.

'Oh, do please! I would be so grateful.'

But where on earth was Fleury-la-Forêt? French addresses consisted, infuriatingly, of the name of the village and a postcode, with no indication of the region; for all she knew the place could be on the Belgian border or halfway up the Pyrenees. Fleury proved on enquiry to be south-west of Orleans, between the Loire and the Cher, only a six- or seven-hour drive from Calais, so she declined Madame de Fleury's offer to send a car to Charles de Gaulle airport to collect her. Her investigations would be more independent if she had her own transport.

She was about to lock up the cottage and hand the key back to the neighbour when she realized guiltily that to dash off at once on her self-appointed mission would be irresponsible. The first priority was to find some other relative to come and sit by old Mrs Greenwood's bedside until her daughter could be found. Somewhere, there must be an address book.

She found it right under her nose by the telephone. Armed with it, she rang Lewes police station, told them that Jane Greenwood seemed to have disappeared, and provided them with the addresses and telephone numbers of three people called Greenwood who could be asked to substitute. When they suggested that she should do the telephoning herself, she resisted the temptation to have a tantrum and explained patiently that she was not a friend of the family or even an acquaintance, that she was dog-tired after a hard day's work and a long drive down to Sussex, and that if the police did not wish to be involved, they could at least pass on a message to the social services in the morning.

'We could do that, madam, certainly. Now, about Dr Greenwood's disappearance. Can you tell me the circumstances?'

She repeated what Adrienne de Fleury had told her.

'And the French police are making enquiries?'

'I believe so, yes.'

'Then we will get in touch through the usual liaison channels, and ask to be informed of the result.'

Having firmly washed her hands of the Greenwood family's affairs, she decided not to confess that she would be off hot-foot on the trail to Fleury in the morning.

Before leaving the cottage, there was one more matter to attend to. Jane Greenwood had been away from home for almost a month. She must have written to her mother. Did her letters contain anything which would give a clue to her disappearance? And had her mother kept them?

She went back to the desk. Distributed among its miscellaneous contents she found a series of long letters written in a firm slightly masculine hand, and signed 'Janey'. At a glance, they seemed to contain nothing sensational, but there was no time to examine them now. She thrust them into her handbag for later study, locked up the cottage, and left.

In the morning she summoned Bill into her office and broke the news that she proposed to slip across to France for a day or two. 'You can manage, can't you?'

'Bit sudden, ain't it?'

'Yes, but I'm exhausted, I need to get away for a bit. So when this friend of my uncle Hugo rang with an invitation, I decided to accept.'

'Seems a bit naughty, going off like that. Celia, you're not on the prowl again after suspects, are you?'

'No, of course not,' she lied, quailing inwardly. She hated deceiving Bill, who was absurdly protective about her. 'Not really,' she added as her conscience smote her.

'Come on Celia, what's all this then?'

She told him, making light of the problem. 'She's probably had a car smash and ended up in hospital. It's sure to be all over by the time I get there.'

'One of these days some naughty villain will land you in hospital, or worse. You should stick to hybridizing hellebores, really you should.'

17

Flushed with adrenalin, she brushed this advice impatiently aside. After a morning of hectic preparations she set off for Dover. She felt strangely invigorated. Her tiredness had given way to excitement, as if she was going on holiday.

TWO

Celia could drive fast when she had to, and the autoroute south from Calais invited speed. But with French time an hour ahead of British, there was no hope of reaching Fleury at a civilized hour. So she stopped north of Paris to spend the night at a quiet family hotel on the banks of the Oise that she had used before. In the rush of departure she had had no time to read Jane Greenwood's letters. But now she took them out of her bag and studied them, in the hope of extracting from them some clue to what had happened to her.

Tuesday 18th May

Dearest Mamma

Well, here I am. The car behaved impeccably despite its age. I lost myself for a time in a tangle of motorways round Paris which are new since that last trip of ours to France five years ago. Even so, I arrived here well before nightfall.

The Château de Fleury is not enormous but very posh, seventeenth century I should think, and built of pale honey-coloured stone. You approach it up a long avenue of limes and through a wrought-iron gateway in a stone screen. Inside the gateway is a paved courtyard. In front of you is the château, with a symmetrical classical frontage and steps leading up to a grand entrance in the middle. To your right is a range of stables, and on the left a kind of open arcade which must have been built

19

to shelter carriages and farm carts. It acts now as a kind of carport for the family's cars. Everything, including the paving of the courtyard, is in the same scrumptious pale stone.

When you get inside, you are confronted with gods and goddesses on the ceilings and a lot of white-painted panelling with gilding on, much of which could do with a good clean. Madame de Fleury received me with the well-drilled charm which I suppose one should expect from a great lady, which she is, every inch of her. Fortunately, she speaks excellent English. You know what my French is like!

Over dinner she asked after Sir Hugo Mackenzie, and seemed disappointed when I had to say that I'd only met him once. She evidently knew him well when they were younger, and started telling me stories about high jinks they'd got up to together in Bucharest and various other outlandish places. From the way she talked about him I wondered if they hadn't been having an affair, anyway he seems to have been quite a lad. When she'd run out of stories about him she started asking me about myself, but I think only because she thought me incapable of conversing on subjects of more general interest, and because it would have been rude not to talk at all.

I spent this morning in the library on the first floor, a handsome room lined with leather-bound books. The botanical drawings I am to work on had been put out for me to see, five huge portfolios of them. They are really outstanding, not just pleasant impressions of the plant such as you find in, for instance Keble Martin, but accurate and elegant drawings in which all the details of leaf and flower shape and colour can be seen, with inserts of pistils, stamens, seed cases, and so on alongside the main illustration. There are usually five or six subjects of

20

the same species or subspecies on each sheet, but they are not properly identified, apart from a few rough scribbles on the backs of the sheets. I am supposed to put all this in order for publication, identifying them will be my job. I still don't understand why Madame de Fleury got me over from England instead of employing someone local, and if there are important differences between the standard French taxonomy and ours, I shall be in trouble. Classifying all this material will take me at least a month, and it worries me that I shall be leaving you for so long. But we do need the money, don't we?

Has Freda answered your letter yet? If she can come and stay for a bit, it will take a great weight off my mind.

Take care of yourself. When you put those ready-frozen meals in the microwave, do make sure they're thoroughly heated through before you eat them and don't forget that Mrs Wilson is calling for you at ten on Wednesday to drive you to the dentist.

With lots of love from your Janey.

The next letter was dated the following day. After discussing possible alternatives if Freda refused to come and hold the fort, Jane gave more details of life at Fleury.

I didn't tell you in my last letter about the other people who live at the château besides the old lady. She occupies the grand bit in the middle, with her son and daughter in the wings on either side of her. The daughter, Chantal, is tall and dark and handsome, a sort of tragedy queen with enormous black eyebrows. She is married to a fat red-faced bull of a man called Emile Marchant, who comes out of their end of the house every morning in a business suit with a briefcase, and drives off to

21

work. Apparently he has a furniture factory in Orleans. He and Chantal have a son, a nice-looking solidly built boy in his twenties, who goes off every day in working clothes but comes back for lunch. Madame de Fleury says he is learning to be a farmer.

Jean-Louis, the son, lives in the other wing of the château. He is tall and slim and wiry, and rather romantic looking with his mother's bright blue eyes and a lot of dark curly hair going nicely grey at the temples. He has a rather lackadaisical manner, but apparently he runs the estate and farms part of it, so the lazy air must be deceptive. He comes and goes all day in a little van which is kept, like the other cars including mine, in the covered arcade at the side of the entrance courtyard which serves as a carport.

Jean-Louis' wife, name of Hortense, is quite a surprise. She is large and very solid, almost square in fact, with elaborately arranged brassy curls of the sort normally found on barmaids. Though nothing has actually been said, I have a feeling that her mother-in-law doesn't like her.

Their daughter is called Anne-Marie, a sweet-looking girl with the same blue eyes and dark curls as her father, and fortunately with his figure rather than her mother's. She is eighteen, has just finished school and will go to university in the autumn.

Madame de Fleury told me before I came that her son's drawings covered the whole of the French flora. But his reference books are still here, and according to one of them, Bonnier and de Layens, there are over five thousand species growing in France, and the drawings cover less than half of them. They will need supplementing with a mass of botanical descriptions if, as she intends, the book is to be issued as a comprehensive guide from which any French wild plant can be identified.

22

Last night at dinner we were joined by Chantal Marchant and Jean-Louis. It was an awkward occasion. They both speak quite reasonable English. But although Madame de Fleury asked them several times to do so for my benefit, they kept lapsing into French and freezing me out of the conversation.

I explained my problem about the botanical drawings and said I couldn't possibly undertake to supply the extra particulars to expand the book into a complete field guide to the French flora. Madame de Fleury seemed disappointed, but I asked if this really mattered? Surely the aim was to publish the drawings of a talented botanist in a form which would be a fitting memorial to him?

Chantal said something in French which sounded fierce and unpleasant, and Jean-Louis made a languid remark, also in French, which obviously upset Madame de Fleury. I turned to her, and she explained. 'They are saying that there is no point in publishing the drawings if they are not complete.'

'Who would buy such a book? No one!' said Chantal, condescending for once to speak English. Jean-Louis spread out his hands in a whimsical gesture which invited his mother to abandon a hopeless venture. She was glaring at them both, angry and disappointed, but they were making no attempt to disguise their pleasure.

Ignoring them, she appealed to me. 'Surely we can arrange something to honour the memory of my poor Paul-Henri? We will discuss this further in the morning.'

An awkward silence fell. To fill the gap in the conversation I said how much I admired the drawings and how sorry I was that such a gifted young botanist should have had his career cut off by one of the banes of modern life, a stupid car accident.

Evidently I had said the wrong thing, not realizing that even eleven years after Paul-Henri's death the wound was still raw. Madame de Fleury became very agitated and dived for her handbag to get out a handkerchief. Jean-Louis laid a hand on her arm and Chantal waved an admonishing finger at me to indicate that this was a taboo subject. I subsided, feeling very embarrassed.

Antoinette began handing the cheese round. When I took some Brie she made a little shocked movement as if I had done something dreadful. While I was still wondering what I'd done wrong, Chantal helped herself to Camembert and immediately spat out a mouthful.

'*Plastique!*' she said accusingly.

This caused an enormous fuss. Chantal glowered under her black eyebrows at Antoinette and Antoinette shook her head in violent denial, with the word '*plastique*' shooting back and forth. Eventually Antoinette stomped out of the room. She came back with the box which had contained the Camembert and plonked it down triumphantly in front of Chantal; the point apparently being that the box was wooden and not, as Chantal had alleged, plastic.

Jean-Louis was thoroughly enjoying her discomfiture, lolling back in his chair and making some mocking remark in French.

'*Animal!*' hissed Chantal, glowering from under her eyebrows at him.

When they had gone home I asked Madame de Fleury what the fuss was all about.

'Oh, it is a stupid mania of Chantal's. You see, when my husband died and the estate was divided up the plantings of poplar trees were part of her share. At that time it was a profitable investment, because all the Camembert boxes were made of poplar wood. But now, most of them are made of plastic, so that the value of the trees is lower, and this is a great grievance to her. She claims that a plastic box gives the cheese an unpleasant taste, and that she can tell the difference. She is usually wrong, but that does not prevent her from making a scene.'

The whole subject of cheese seemed to be fraught with complications, what with Antoinette's horrified reaction when I helped myself. So I asked Madame de Fleury what I had done to upset her.

'Oh, unfortunately poor Antoinette does not quite realize that foreigners can't always follow our complicated conventions. French people consider, rightly or wrongly, that the centre of a Brie is the most succulent part. So it is considered very shocking to cut off the pointed end of the wedge, as you did, instead of taking a piece from the side so that the specially nice bit at the end is shared between everyone at the table.'

I apologized, and said I hoped that if I did anything else which violated French sensibilities she would tell me. She replied that since I had asked, I might care to know that it was considered impolite during meals to let one's hands lie in one's lap when not actually eating; they must always be visible above the table.

Why, I wonder? When I went to bed, I decided that having holidays in France teaches one nothing whatever about the French people.

In the morning Madame de Fleury came up to the library, and we looked at the portfolios of drawings together. 'You say that the drawings are not complete? You're sure?'

'Quite sure, Madame.'

'But he told me that his work was almost finished. He had made specimens of almost all the savage flowers of France.'

I said nothing. It was not for me to point out that

her beloved Paul-Henri must have lied to her.

She stared at the drawings for a moment. 'This is not the whole of his work. There is something else.'

She went to the gap in the shelves from which the portfolios of drawings had been taken, then ranged round the room in search of whatever she thought was missing. 'There were a great many *chemises*, what do you call them? Folders, I think. They were full of flowers, dried and pressed, thousands of them. But where are these folders?'

I was intrigued. If there was a complete collection of dried herbarium specimens, it altered the whole situation.

Antoinette was summoned, and asked if she knew where the folders were. This was of course in French. But she obviously knew, because we all processed up to the garrets in the roof and began searching through the sort of débris one finds in attics: broken-down furniture, children's cots, disused bedroom china, old sports gear. Ranging through all this Antoinette homed in on an enormous, dilapidated cabin trunk whose days of travel were long over, and opened it.

'There they are!' cried Madame de Fleury.

There were several hundred of the folders. It took Antoinette and me an hour to carry them all downstairs to the library. I opened one of them. The herbarium specimens were in perfect condition, and labelled in a neat, scholarly hand with the Latin name and the place and date of collection. After consulting Antoinette, Madame de Fleury explained that they had been in Paul-Henri's room when he died. The room was cleared and they had been stored in the attic because there was no room for them in the library. 'With their help, perhaps you could supply descriptions of the species not illustrated by the drawings.'

26

I said I would let her know after I had examined the specimens at greater leisure. But a quick check established that they covered the French flora far more thoroughly. It looks to me as if the project can go ahead.

It became clear from the next letter that Freda was unable to come and stay with Mrs Greenwood to hold the fort. Jane urged her to invite Angela as a substitute rather than Winifred, 'who eats such a lot and is rather scatty'. Then she went on to describe progress with her botanical problem.

I have discovered a copy of the *Flora Europaea* among Paul-Henri's reference books. So I have told Madame de Fleury that with it and the herbarium specimens to guide me, I could probably fill out the book so that it becomes a complete guide to the French flora. But Paul-Henri de Fleury died in 1983, so all his reference books are out of date and in the interval taxonomy has moved on. I told Madame de Fleury that I would need to consult a qualified French botanist from time to time. But she was a bit tiresome and obstructive about that, and said there was no hurry. It would be best if I made a note of all my queries, so that they could be submitted together to some competent authority at the end. I still don't understand why she didn't commission a French person in the first place.

All this means a lot of extra work which of course will also mean more badly needed money. But I'm worried about leaving you to your own devices for even longer than we planned.

This morning when Emile Marchant and Jean-Louis de Fleury were getting out their cars to go off to work, they started making remarks to each other across the courtyard, with Emile bellowing

and Jean-Louis being relaxed and sarcastic as usual.
After a time, both wives came out of their
respective ends of the house, and the shouting
match became a foursome. French people often
seem to address each other in loud voices, and it
did not occur to me at the time that they might be
quarrelling. But this evening, just before dinner,
Chantal marched into the salon in a high old state,
followed by her husband looking even more bull-
like and determined than usual. She snatched some
papers from him and brandished them under
Madame de Fleury's nose. Then hot on their heels
in came Jean-Louis looking like Lord Byron in a
bad temper, with his fat brassy Hortense waddling
along behind him.

A furious row broke out, with Chantal behaving
like a dissatisfied tigress and Jean-Louis sounding
laid back, like men do when they think a woman is
being unreasonable, and refusing to take the
papers which she was thrusting at him. Then
Hortense and Chantal rounded on poor Madame
de Fleury and made her look at the papers, which
were obviously bills, as if they expected her to pay
them. But by that stage I was withdrawing tactfully
to leave them to it.

It strikes me as odd that Chantal and Jean-Louis,
who are both thin and dark, should have married
very fat, fair people. Or rather, Hortense's curls
could have been any colour before she got to work
on them. But Emile's carroty bristles are obviously
natural.

When they had gone and calm had been restored
I reappeared, to find Madame de Fleury looking
very shaken, but trying to make light of the fracas.
'Oh dear, what a tohu-bohu,' she said with a serio-
comic gesture. 'When an inheritance is divided there
are always quarrels about money, but I see no
reason why they should expect me to arbitrate.'

28

During dinner she and Antoinette kept
exchanging rather agitated little remarks in French
like two hens who have seen a fox.

The next letter expressed relief that Angela had agreed
to stay with the old lady for a fortnight, then reported
steady progress on the botanical front.

The Ranunculaceae are a huge and unwieldy family,
but as I told you, the herbarium specimens are
meticulously labelled, and I have polished them off
already and romped through the Berberidaceae
and the Nymphaeaceae. I've just started on the
Papaveraceae which are much the same as ours
apart from a few Mediterranean and Alpine species.
I am collecting quite a lot of taxonomic problems.
It doesn't matter enormously when the herbarium
labelling follows Scopini rather than Crantz and
talks about *Glaucium luteum* instead of *Glaucium
flavum*, but it worries me when he writes *Anemone
pulsatilla* following Linnaeus, though Miller has
established quite clearly that the *Pulsatillas* are a
completely separate species from the anemones.
  The weather is getting very hot, and Madame de
Fleury and I often have our after-lunch coffee on
the terrace on the shady side of the house. There is
no proper flower garden, only a lawn below the
terrace, enclosed in a circle of clipped hornbeam
hedges set about with statues, and it has a round
ornamental pool in the middle. For the past few
days a young gardener has been trimming the
hedges. He usually wears nothing at work but
sandals and a pair of shorts. He is blond and very
well set up, with wide shoulders and a narrow waist
and the sort of muscles you see on Greek and
Roman statues. He is obviously very proud of his
physique, and struts around with his chest thrust
out like a turkey-cock. Madame de Fleury says he

29

is the son of Antoinette Dupont, the housekeeper, and his name is Philippe.

Yesterday he came up on to the terrace while we were having coffee, and spoke to Madame de Fleury in what seemed to me a very familiar tone. I gathered from his gestures that he was asking if he could have some coffee. She refused very curtly, and I think told him to go and put his shirt on. He went, but only after helping himself to a lump of sugar from the coffee tray and making a retort which sounded to me very impertinent. All this seemed to me very odd behaviour for a gardener.

Meanwhile, being cooped up indoors during this lovely weather is very frustrating, and I have devised a wicked scheme. Do you remember how I used to weep buckets as a girl over a book translated from the French, *Le Grand Meaulnes* by Alain-Fournier? It's set in a wild, lonely area of woodland and heath about twelve miles south of here, called the Sologne. To judge from the map, it's full of little pools and lakes, and it's well known to botanists specializing in bryophytes for the richness and variety of its mosses. One day soon I shall invent some story about having to do field work and go and have a look.

Had Jane Greenwood carried out this plan? According to Adrienne de Fleury she had disappeared while on a field trip connected with her work on Paul-Henri's botanical drawings. It looked as if she had told her a lie, gone into the Sologne, and met with some misadventure. But the Sologne was a huge area, where should one start looking for clues?

The rest of the letter contained an attempt to unravel the tangled relationships at Fleury.

I wish I understood the position in the household of Antoinette's son Philippe. For a gardener, he seems to be on surprisingly familiar terms with

30

everybody. The other day, it was stiflingly hot and I went to the library window for a breath of air. While I was there Anne-Marie, Madame de Fleury's enchantingly pretty granddaughter, came out of the house to feed the goldfish in the ornamental pool. Philippe was up on a step-ladder cutting the hornbeam hedge. When he saw her he got down from his ladder, came up quite close to her and began to chat. For a moment or two she and this half-naked man were only a few inches apart. She stepped back smartly but went on talking to him in quite a friendly way. I do hope she is not attracted to him. She is far too young and he is obviously a rampant tomcat. After a few minutes of this her mother, Jean-Louis' brassy-haired wife, came rushing out of her end of the house to break it up. He gave her a very impudent look, and tried to lead Anne-Marie away with him, but I was glad to see that she did not go. He seems to have a privileged position of some kind. I wonder why.

This evening another mystery presented itself. A rough-looking man in working clothes and the sort of peaked cap that peasants here wear came into the courtyard and stationed himself, obviously drunk, outside the Marchants' wing of the château, shouting what sounded like abuse. After a time Emile Marchant came out and started shouting back. When the man refused to go away Emile, who was much the heavier and more powerful of the two, started knocking him about really savagely, and ended by turning him round and giving him a kick on the behind which landed him flat on his face. Not content with this Emile pulled him to his feet and half dragged, half carried him across the courtyard to the exit gateway. It seemed to me an unnecessarily brutal way of dealing with a drunk.

As I sat writing this in my room, someone started

playing a guitar down on the terrace. I looked out, and there in the twilight were Anne-Marie and her cousin André under the windows of Jean-Louis' end of the château. As I watched, they started singing a sort of serenade to her parents, quite a spirited song with a strong rhythm. They were making rather a noise and after a time a window opened and Anne-Marie's mother leaned out, screaming what sounded like abuse. They stopped singing at once, laughed and moved away. It seemed a bit ungracious of Hortense, even if their serenade disturbed her. After all, it wasn't really late.

It became clear from the next letter that old Mrs Greenwood had decided to manage alone when Angela left, rather than invite scatty Winifred with her enormous appetite. Jane expressed cautious approval of this decision, then reported on the previous evening's events.

Last night Madame de Fleury invited Anne-Marie and André to dinner, to practise their English, she said. She obviously dotes on her grandchildren, and they are certainly a handsome pair. In the daytime they both wear the dismal collections of rags which seem to be the ultimate in youthful chic, but they had both dressed formally for dinner, and looked very smart. They have beautiful manners, and although their English is a bit stiff and hesitant they chatted away to me conscientiously.

I made one embarrassing gaffe during dinner. They were discussing some rally that Anne-Marie's mother wanted her to attend, though she did not. I assumed from what they were saying that it was a political rally, and remarked that different generations did not always see eye to eye where politics were involved. There were some quickly suppressed giggles at this, and Madame de Fleury explained that the *rallye* in question (it is spelt with an E at the end) was not political, but one of a number of clubs run by aristocratic hostesses, who give parties at which young people of the best families can meet each other in pleasant circumstances.

During all this André and Anne-Marie were making a curious gesture, rubbing the knuckles of one hand up and down against the side of their faces. Madame de Fleury saw I was puzzled, and explained. Apparently there's a slang expression 'it's razor', meaning that something is very boring, and when people mime the action of shaving they are silently saying the same thing. Why the French connect razors with boredom I can't imagine.

Anne-Marie insisted that the parties were 'mortally boring'. Apparently the only young men admitted were sprigs of the nobility with nothing much between the ears, and most of the girls were just as bad, the real point being to discourage young people of the best families from consorting with undesirables. I asked her what sort of thing got one kept out as an undesirable.

'Simple,' said Anne-Marie. 'You are kept out if you do not have a *particule.*'

Madame de Fleury explained that a *particule* was the 'de' which members of old-established families have in front of their names.

'Yes,' said Anne-Marie. 'I am invited to the Comtesse de Mirecourt's *rallye* because I am de Fleury de Marcilly, but André cannot go because he is not de anything but plain André Marchant. Without him I shan't go. No and no and no!'

At this André gave her a really beautiful smile across the table. Any suggestion of romance between first cousins is worrying, but at least André is an improvement on Philippe Dupont, the half-naked muscle-man.

Madame de Fleury did not try very hard to make Anne-Marie change her mind. After they had gone she said that she saw little point nowadays in noble families holding themselves aloof, and anyway the state did not recognize their titles. When I asked her if she herself had a title she said, 'Of course, but why insist?'

According to her, Anne-Marie will have to attend the party because her mother has social ambitions for her and takes the 'rallyes' very seriously; 'but of course my daughter-in-law comes from a different background from ours'.

The brassy-haired Hortense certainly seemed to me rather common, but this is the first time I have seen Madame de Fleury with her claws out.

It appeared from the next letter that there had been a misunderstanding between old Mrs Greenwood and the milkman, which her next door neighbour had dealt with tactfully. Then came a fresh insight into the mystery of the presumptuous, too-handsome Philippe.

One of his jobs is to collect any letters that Madame de Fleury has written, and take them to catch the afternoon post in the village. Yesterday when he came into the salon to collect them I was suddenly struck by the resemblance between him and the portrait of Madame de Fleury's husband, also a very handsome man, which hangs over the fireplace. If Philippe is his natural son by the maid Antoinette, that would account for his rather arrogant behaviour. I wonder if I'm right.

Unfortunately Madame de Fleury caught me looking from Philippe to the portrait and comparing them. She was not at all pleased.

I told you in my last letter about my wicked plan to escape into the Sologne. This morning I put it into effect. I told her that waterlily flowers were too

34

fat and juicy to make good herbarium specimens,
and I needed to do some field work on them in the
pools and lakes of the Sologne. Soon after
breakfast I set off there in search of my bryophytes,
taking with me A. E. Smith's *Moss Flora of Britain
and Ireland*.

But the Sologne was a bitter disappointment. I
had expected to be able to wander over vast
expanses of bog and heath dotted with ponds and
lakes, but not a bit of it. The area has changed
completely since Alain-Fournier's day, and has not
been spared development, because it is near
enough to Paris to be dotted with second homes. A
lot of the land to either side of the main roads has
been fenced off and the tracks leading into it all
have notices saying that they are private or lead
to this or that château. There are also a lot of boards
reading '*chasse gardée*', which means that the
shooting rights are reserved.

Presumably the ponds are still there, but most of
them are hidden away inside these estates, which
I found frustrating because their margins provide
the habitats of the mosses I would most like to
study. I drove about for a time without finding
anything resembling a suitable moss habitat. Then
I went into a village shop and tried unsuccessfully
to buy a guide book to the region in English. But
a couple who were in the shop spoke some English
and we got into conversation. When I told them
how disappointed I was to find that all the lakes
and pools were privately owned, they suggested
that I should go to the Château de Ciran near by,
where the estate is open to the public as a kind of
theme park, so that one can study nature and see
what the Sologne must have been like before so
much of it was enclosed. I went there in high hopes,
but was again bitterly disappointed. The château
was very ugly, rather like a Victorian shooting lodge

in Scotland, and the emphasis in the park was on bird and animal life rather than the flora. There were a number of quite large pools, but they were covered with waterfowl and the banks had been maintained for the convenience of visitors wanting to view them, leaving nothing resembling a moss habitat.

So I went away feeling rather downcast, and was driving around in despair when I suddenly saw a sandy track leading off the road into the woodland. The land to either side of the track was fenced off, and I could see another ugly shooting-lodge type château in the woods on the corner, but there was no notice saying the track was private. So I drove up it for about a mile and came on a cluster of promising little pools. There were notices everywhere saying '*chasse gardée*' and a track leading off past the pools claimed to be a '*chemin privé*', but there was no one about so I parked the car and hopped over the fence to explore. One of the larger pools contained just what I was looking for, an area of bare mud at one end where the water had receded. It had been colonized by a whole variety of mosses including *Calligeron cuspidatum* and *Ephemerum serratum* and *Brachythecium rivulare* and *Bryum bicolor* and goodness knows what else, and there were some liverworts too, mostly *Riccardia* species. By this time it was getting late. So I collected specimens of as many as I could to take home. After dinner I retired to my room pleading 'a slight headache' and spent a happy evening dissecting my finds and determining them under the microscope. I'm glad I brought it with me, for the minute differences between e.g. the various *Bryums* would have been impossible to detect with a hand glass. Anyway the results of my examination were quite fascinating. I even found a *Physcomitrium* of a variety which was definitely other than *pyriforme*, the only species found in the British Isles. I shall certainly have to go back to that pool when opportunity offers.

Had Jane gone back there? Celia wondered. Probably. According to Madame de Fleury she had disappeared while claiming to be engaged on field work for the book. In pursuit of her obsession with mosses and liverworts she had trespassed on private land, and this might have got her into trouble. But it was quite possible that her misadventure, whatever it was, had happened elsewhere. Nevertheless, the obvious starting point of any investigation would be this pool somewhere not too far from the Château de Ciran in the Sologne.

But had Jane gone back to exactly the same spot, as she intended? This question was answered in her next letter. It was the last, dated on the Friday, two days before she died.

Hortense has decided to spend a few days at a spa, as part of a very necessary campaign to get her weight down. Madame de Fleury has decided to go with her, although of course she has no weight problem. She says she needs a change of air, but I have a horrid feeling that she gets very bored by having to make conversation to me at our mealtimes together, and has seized on this excuse to escape.

Anyway this development has left me free to come and go to the Sologne as I wish, and I have just spent the day by my pool there. I was specially anxious to sort out the *Bryums*. The specific boundaries in that family are very finely drawn, especially between *caespicitum* and *cappillare*, and I suspect that the varieties here differ from the British ones. I parked the car as before at the side of the sandy track and nipped over the fence, and had been hard at work for an hour when a man with a gun appeared from behind the trees and

37

shouted something. I tried to explain what I was
doing, but he obviously didn't understand English
and came right up to me looking very fierce and
gesturing to me to go back over the fence. I showed
him my copy of Smith's *Moss Flora of Britain and
Ireland*, which obviously meant nothing to him. But
when I pointed to the moss colony and showed
him the specimens I had taken from it and my hand
glass, he seemed to grasp what I was up to. He
scratched his head and looked amused, and in the
end made signs that it was all right, and I could
carry on with what I was doing. But he made
gestures to indicate that I was not to go any further
into the woods.

Who was the man with the gun? He would have to be
found and interviewed. But this was not the end of the
letter.

Madame de Fleury has arranged for me to have my
meals with the Marchants while she is away, which
is sensible because it gives Antoinette a break. It is
all rather a strain. André, who is really a very nice
boy, did his best to talk a bit to me, but was rather
put off by his parents, who kept including him in
their conversation in French. They are all three
meticulous about keeping their hands above table
level between the courses, and I try to remember
and follow their example. But I have noticed that
it does not seem to matter how you drink your soup.
Instead of sucking it quietly from the side of the
spoon as we do, you can put the end in your mouth
as if you were a sword-swallower, and nobody
worries if you make a noise.
    The Marchant's bit of the château is much less
grand than Madame de Fleury's. There is no
panelling and gilding on the walls and no allegorical
paintings on the ceilings.

This morning I decided to walk to the village to buy more stamps. As I was setting off Chantal Marchant came hurrying out of her end of the house and said she wanted to come too. I naturally agreed, whereupon she indicated that she wanted me to drive her there in the Mini. It is only about half a mile so I was a bit surprised, but she is not the sort of lady one says 'no' to. So I went to get the Mini out from under its shelter, and as I reached it Philippe, half-naked as usual, materialized from nowhere and took the keys from me and unlocked it with a flourish. He managed somehow to do this while displaying himself like a huge bird in full breeding plumage.

Chantal got in beside me and we drove to the village. I got my stamps, then realized why she had wanted to go in the car. She was doing an enormous shop, with masses of potatoes and vegetables and detergents and things in tins, much more than she could have carried home on foot. She loaded all this into the Mini and then, just as we were setting off, the awful-looking peasant that Mr Marchant had seen off the premises so brutally came up alongside and shouted something which sounded very nasty. Chantal shouted something back and wound up the window, but was not quick enough and the spittle hit her on the cheek. To avoid further trouble I drove away at once, longing to know what this was all about.

'He is mad, that is all,' said Chantal, glaring at me from under the fearsome eyebrows.

'Or just drunk?' I queried.

'Don't you understand, he is mad,' she repeated in a voice of thunder which forbade further questioning. Is the man nursing some grudge against her and her husband? That is what it looks like.

I really must concentrate more on the botanical drawings, which I have neglected shamefully of late. But I am getting very discouraged by the difficulty of working within a foreign taxonomy which differs in important detail from our own. When I was approached to do the job by Madame de Fleury, I decided that I couldn't afford to look a gift horse in the mouth, but why on earth did she get me over from England instead of taking on someone local? I decided yesterday that I couldn't continue till I had got some authoritative advice about up-to-date French opinion on the arrangement of species and genera. The obvious place to look to was a university with a botany department, so this afternoon I drove boldly into the centre of Orleans, managed to locate the university, and made a student who spoke some English guide me to the right building. Fortunately the professor (I think that was what he was) spoke excellent English and was very helpful, providing some very interesting information which I will tell you about when I have investigated the matter in greater detail.

Meanwhile, the atmosphere here has suddenly become very tense. When I arrived at the Marchants at the usual dinner time I heard voices raised in a furious quarrel in the living-room, much more violent than anything I had heard before. The Marchants were shouting wildly at someone who was answering back in a voice I didn't recognize, a harsh, almost hysterical screech. I stood in the hall listening for a time, not wishing to intrude but wondering when, if at all, I would get any dinner. Then, before I could decide what to do, Jean-Louis de Fleury flung out of the room, completely transformed. He was dead white. His nostrils were pinched and his brilliant blue eyes had turned into narrow slits in his fury.

I waited a little to let the Marchants calm down, then walked in. Chantal and her husband stood facing each other in a kind of rigid daze, and poor

André was staring at them, looking very white.
There was no one else in the room. Only then did
I realize that the person screeching hysterically
must have been Jean-Louis.

After that, dinner was of course very
uncomfortable. No one said a word to me
throughout the meal. The grown-ups kept muttering
angrily to each other in French. André was looking
too upset to eat, and Emile gulped his food down
furiously in a way that made me fear for his
digestion.

I left the table as soon as I could, and am writing
this in the library, which is cooler than my bedroom
in this rather trying weather. Just now voices down
on the terrace outside floated up through the open
window. Another quarrel was going on, and when I
investigated I saw to my distress that it was
between André Marchant and pretty little Anne-
Marie de Fleury. It's obvious that the relations
between the two sets of parents are not what they
should be, but the quarrelling seems to have
extended to the next generation. Why are those two
nice young people at loggerheads? Up to now they
have been so very close. Has some new bone of
contention presented itself and engulfed the
whole family?

Look after yourself, Mother, and do make sure
you heat things thoroughly in the microwave
before you eat them.

Love, Janey.

That was the last letter in the series. Was Jane Greenwood
right? Was there a new bone of contention, to be added
to the long list of mysteries that had perplexed her at
Fleury? Wondering about this, Celia put the letters back
in her handbag, then settled down to sleep. But sleep
did not come quickly. She had too many questions on
her mind.

41

THREE

Reviewing the situation in the morning, Celia decided that Jane Greenwood's letters threw very little light on what had happened to her. The hectic carry-on of the family at Fleury was a mass of riddles, but Jane was not involved in it except as a bewildered spectator. The clue to the mystery probably lay in the Sologne, and it was there that the investigation would have to start. From the details she had provided, it should at least be possible to locate the pool where she had spent hours drooling over her dreary little bits of moss. Taking the theme park at the Château de Ciran as the starting point, one would drive round the nearby area looking for a wide sandy track leading off the road, with an ugly château in a wood near the entrance. The pool would be somewhere up this track, near a private drive leading off it into the woods.

Pinpointing the spot might not get the investigation anywhere. Misadventure might have overtaken Jane elsewhere, on the way to her pool or on the way back. Nor was there any guarantee that she had gone back to the same spot. Nevertheless it was worth trying, and on reflection Celia saw no reason why she should leave the pleasure of finding the right place to the police. She would go straight to the Sologne in the morning, and get the job over before she presented herself at the Château de Fleury and got involved in its complex family politics.

Before leaving she telephoned Madame de Fleury to say that she would arrive in the late afternoon if that was convenient, and set off again down the autoroute. After

a struggle with the tangle of inadequately signposted free-
ways which skirted round·Paris, she headed on south and
arrived at La Ferté-Saint-Aubin in the Sologne in time
for an early lunch.

Having eaten, she bought a large-scale map of the area
in the local Syndicat d'Initiative and set off to try to find
Jane's pool; and if possible the man with the gun who had
encountered her there. Instead of driving into the grounds
of the Château de Ciran she explored the quiet side roads
surrounding its park, without at first finding anything corresponding to Jane's description of the layout. But when
she cast her net wider, suddenly there it was: the sandy
track leading off the road into the woods, and on the
corner a château dimly visible among the trees. She drove
up the track, flanked on either side by notice after notice
to the effect that the shooting was preserved. Several
drives led off it into the woods, with the information that
they were private phrased in various ways, but there was
no sign of water near by. Then a little further on, she
found it, a sunlit pond glimmering through the trees, and
a drive leading off from the track with a dilapidated board
reading '*chemin privé*'. Further up the drive there was an
even more dilapidated notice to the effect that this was
the drive of the Château des Étangs.

Reflecting that Jane would have saved her a great deal
of trouble if she had vouchsafed this last detail to her
mother, Celia parked, climbed over the wire fence, and
reconnoitred. There, sure enough, was the area of drying
mud at the end of the pond, half covered with the mosses
and liverworts which Jane had found so engrossing; and
among them, rather movingly, her footprints in the mud.

A search revealed nothing else to give a clue to her
disappearance, so Celia returned to her car and drove up
the private track towards the château, hoping to find the
dwelling of the man with the gun. What she found was a
shooting lodge in the worst possible nineteenth-century
taste, standing in a clearing which also contained a large
pool teeming with waterfowl. She repressed a twinge of

disgust. Frightening ducks up into the air and shooting them had never seemed to her a legitimate form of sport.

It was not the shooting season and the lodge seemed deserted, with its shutters closed. But her arrival had unleashed the fury of some dogs, whose baying seemed to come from a tumbledown cottage on the edge of the clearing. She went up to it and heard, half drowned by the noise the dogs were making, a sound of someone chopping wood. She called. A voice told the dogs harshly to be quiet and its owner, a heavily built man with a two-day growth of beard, appeared round the corner of the cottage.

'Madame?'

Celia explained that she was enquiring after a lady botanist who had been working in the area during the previous week. '*Vous l'avez vue, Monsieur? Une dame anglaise.*'

'Oh! That one.' Certainly he had seen her, and he did not attempt to hide his amusement. He painted a lively picture of Jane hunched down at the edge of the pool, inspecting its contents alertly like a heron on the watch for fish. 'She is a friend of yours, madame?'

'An acquaintance only.'

'I understood in the end what she was doing, though she spoke no French, not a word. But when I approached her, and she showed me her miserable little shreds of greenery, I thought at first that she was completely *toquée*.'

'One has to be a bit *toquée* to be as interested as that in mosses. When did you last see her here?'

He frowned. 'I am not certain. Why do you ask?'

'She has disappeared. She failed to return from one of her botanical expeditions.'

'How unfortunate. I am sorry.'

'It is important to establish when she was last seen.'

'Let me see. I remember now. It was last Sunday. She was there, crouching in the mud at the end of the pool, when I drove past on my way to mass. I waved to her, but she was too absorbed to notice me.'

'At what time? Can you remember?'

'Just before eleven o'clock. The mass in La Ferté is at eleven, and I was rather late because I had to feed the dogs first and go round the cages of the young pheasants. She was there when I went, but when I came back after the mass her car was not there and there was no sign of her.'

'Thank you, Monsieur. It is evident that if something has happened to her, it happened after she left here. But there will have to be a police inquiry, and I regret that it may be necessary for them to trouble you. So may I have your name?'

His name was Etienne Lamotte, he said, and talking to the police would not trouble him, he was in good relations with them. As for the lady, it was clear, was it not, Madame, that she was ever so slightly *dingue*, in which case irrational disappearances from time to time were to be expected. He saw every hope that she would turn up unharmed.

On this cheerful note they parted.

On looking at the map, Celia realized that she was quite a long way from Fleury, and set off there through quiet country lanes. When she drove up the avenue of limes and through the ornamental gateway of the château, she saw at once that Jane Greenwood had not exaggerated its attractions. It was not enormous, but perfectly proportioned. The main building, the courtyard, and the flanking buildings to either side formed a balanced composition, made irresistible by the warm honey-coloured stone.

She parked under the covered arcade described in Jane's letters, crossed to the great door in the centre of the façade, and rang the bell. A woman in her forties with faded fair hair answered.

'*Bonsoir, Madame*,' she said. '*Je suis l'amie anglaise de Miss Greenwood.*'

Antoinette nodded and smiled. '*Madame est dans le jardin. Par içi, s'il vous plaît.*'

45

Celia followed her through an echoing hall with faded gods and goddesses on the high ceiling and out through open French doors on to a terrace at the far side of the house.

Adrienne de Fleury rose to greet her. She was not alone, and embarked on introductions. But Celia had already recognized the other members of Jane's cast of characters: dark, romantic-looking Jean-Louis de Fleury with his languid charm and his mother's bright blue eyes; his fat wife Hortense with her plain pink-and-white face and her brassy curls; his sister Chantal, the tragedy queen with the swarthy eyebrows; and Emile Marchant, her red-faced bull-like husband with his prominent eyes and short-cropped reddish hair. Celia sensed that she had interrupted something. There was tension in the air. Adrienne was fingering her lip nervously. Chantal and the two men seemed to be choking back anger.

But her presence meant that these emotions had to be switched off. What was switched on was the calm behaviour and relaxed conversation appropriate to receiving a guest. Nobody remarked on Celia's fluent and reasonably correct French. This was an accomplishment which properly educated people of whatever nationality were expected to have mastered.

At Adrienne's request Jean-Louis explained what had been done so far to trace Miss Greenwood. He had reported that she was missing to the local gendarmerie. But they had pointed out that as she had left everything behind in her room, this suggested that she had not disappeared by her own wish. For that reason the affair was now in the hands of the criminal police in Orleans. Perhaps Madame Grant did not know, but under the French legal system they were under the supervision of an examining magistrate or Juge d'Instruction, and were therefore known as the Police Judiciaire.

As it happened Madame Grant did know, and said she would make contact with them.

'Do, Celia,' said Adrienne, 'go and push those useless people to do something.'

'It will be my first priority in the morning, Madame.'

'Oh, do call me Adrienne, please! The police are so flooded over with crime that they don't know where to point their heads, unless one goes there and makes a noise, they display no energy.'

Jean-Louis went on to say that he had given them a description of Jane's car, but not its registration number, which no one at Fleury could remember. Celia felt guilty. She should have armed herself with the number before leaving England.

'The *immatriculation* of the car is not important,' said Jean-Louis casually. 'If it is seen, it will be recognized at once.'

'Yes,' added Emile. 'It's a crazy car, the size of a child's toy and bright red, with the steering-wheel on the wrong side.'

'And very old, with scratches on the paint,' added Hortense. 'It has perhaps broken down finally somewhere on the road.'

'True,' said Adrienne. 'Driving that old *bagnole*, she has probably had an accident.'

'No, *Maman*,' Jean-Pierre explained wearily, as if to a stupid child. 'I told you, remember? No traffic accident has been reported, and no one answering her description has been admitted to a hospital.'

Adrienne frowned. 'It is quite a mystery, this disappearance. Jean-Louis, you are sure she did not say where she was going?'

'Quite sure, *Maman*.' His ultra-patient tone suggested that she was senile and losing her memory. 'I have told you many times. She said only that she would pursue her botanical researches in the Sologne.'

'But where in the Sologne?' she insisted, but he only shrugged.

'Researches into what?' demanded Chantal acidly. 'Paul-Henri had completed his work on the flora, there

47

was nothing more to do. But while you and Hortense were away, *Maman*, she crept away from here quietly several times. Why?'

'Went to meet some bloke, I bet,' said Emile, 'a type she'd picked up in some bar, and he was one of these shocking perverts who kill women.'

'Disgusting!' snapped Hortense.

'I always knew this business would end in disaster,' murmured Jean-Louis.

Adrienne rounded on him. 'You foresaw that when I arranged for Paul-Henri's drawings to be published a mortally boring Englishwoman would be murdered?'

'Raped and murdered,' corrected Emile. His bulging eyes glittered at the prospect.

'There's no reason to assume that she's dead,' Celia protested.

'Nevertheless a sordid adventure with some man is a possibility,' Chantal insisted. 'She was very sensible to the attractions of men. When Philippe Dupont was parading his torso in the garden, she could not tear away her eyes from him.'

There hung in the air, unspoken, the French belief that Englishwomen travelling abroad alone tended as a class to throw prudery to the winds and give free rein to uninhibited Anglo-Saxon lust.

Celia decided to put a stop to this line of speculation. 'There is no mystery about where she went. She's a botanist who specializes in mosses, and she crept off to the Sologne to study the local ones.'

Cries of incredulous dismay greeted this.

'How dare she?' Hortense snorted with indignation. 'She was supposed to be arranging those drawings, that was what *Maman* paid her for, not crawling about the Sologne looking for moss.'

'I know,' said Celia. 'It was naughty of her, but not as naughty as promiscuous sex with men in bars.'

'How do you know it was moss and not men in bars?' demanded Emile.

'She mentioned her studies in the Sologne in her letters to her mother. And she made no mention in them of meeting men.'

Jean-Louis permitted himself a wry smile. 'If you had become acquainted with a louche seducer in a bar, would you mention the circumstance in your letters to your mother?'

To this Celia had no ready answer.

'You have seen these letters, my dear Celia?' Adrienne asked.

'I have them here in my bag, and shall hand them to the police when I see them in Orleans tomorrow, but they contain nothing which throws light on her disappearance. They are mostly about her botanical work and her observations of life here at Fleury.'

'Observations?' Adrienne echoed. 'It would interest me to see what opinions that poor stupid woman formed of us.'

Celia hesitated. 'Some of her remarks are rather unflattering.'

'In that case I am all the more interested,' said Adrienne.

Celia produced the bundle of letters from her bag and spread them on the garden table. Adrienne picked one up. Chantal and Emile Marchant and Jean-Louis de Fleury also took one each and began reading. Hortense picked one up, but felt obliged to show how well bred she was by making polite conversation to Celia instead of reading it.

As the readers exchanged the pages among themselves, differing reactions became apparent. Jean-Louis seemed quietly amused. Emile read solidly, but showed no reaction. Chantal snorted with indignation every time she turned a page.

'It is all lies!' she shouted, then came on some fresh cause of outrage. 'Oh, what is this, how dare she?'

Hortense abandoned her conversation with Celia and began reading intently.

Adrienne's progress through the letters was marked by little exclamations of pleasure, as if she was enjoying Jane's sallies against the rest of the household. 'She is less stupid than I thought, my dear Celia. She even perceived that I found her mortally boring. I can't tell you what I went through trying to find subjects of conversation at mealtimes. She is quite right, in the end I went off to that spa with Hortense because I couldn't tolerate it any more.'

'These letters cannot be shown to the police,' thundered Chantal frowning. 'She exaggerates, none of it is true. We do not spend our time sticking poisoned knives into each other.'

'Don't we?' grunted Emile.

'The picture she paints is remarkably accurate,' agreed Jean-Louis.

'You have all brought disgrace on the name of Fleury by your behaviour,' proclaimed Hortense loftily. 'I am ashamed of our family.'

'It's not your family, except by marriage,' snapped Chantal, 'so shut your mouth and don't give yourself airs.' She snatched up a handful of pages from the table. 'There will be no disgrace, we will burn all this at once. The police must not see it.'

'I'm afraid they must,' said Celia.

They looked at her, as if they had forgotten she was there.

'One of the letters contains the information they will need to identify the spot she visited in the Sologne. It is there that the investigation will have to start.'

'Then give them that letter and destroy the rest,' Jean-Louis suggested languidly.

Celia picked up the letter in question. 'She says here that she mentioned her plan to visit the Sologne in a previous letter. It's obvious that this one forms part of a series. If we suppress the others they'll suspect that we're concealing something.'

'Why should they?' asked Emile.

'You yourself suggested that there might have been an

entanglement with some man. The police must be allowed to see that there's no hint of such a thing.'

'I still say everything must all be destroyed,' Chantal insisted.

'I'm sorry, I can't allow that,' said Celia. 'I'm here to represent the interests of Miss Greenwood's family, and I must give the police every help in their efforts to find her.'

'*Maman*, can you not prevent this horror?' demanded Hortense.

'No,' said Adrienne grimly. 'Celia is within her rights. I would have preferred to wash our dirty linen in the family and not in the commissariat de police. But since some of you chose to indulge in these *chamailleries* in front of a stranger, we must all bear the consequences. And now perhaps, Celia, you would like to be shown your room, and refresh yourself before dinner?'

Celia agreed, gathered up the letters and withdrew, leaving ominous tensions behind her.

Philippe, summoned by Antoinette from their flat above the stables, appeared to fetch her bag from her car and take it up to her room. In the cool of the early evening he was hiding his main attractions in slacks and a sweater, but his Eau de Cologne, his expensive-looking blond haircut, and his very white teeth, regular but slightly too numerous, were very much in evidence.

Her room was furnished in heavy nineteenth-century mahogany, with rugs on the bare boards of the floor. It looked out over the entrance courtyard. She realized that Jane's room must have been on the other side of the house, since she had used it as an observation post from which to spy on events down on the terrace. When she had unpacked and changed, she decided to have a look at it and explored. After peeping into Adrienne's boudoir and bedroom, and a primitive bathroom, she found a room containing clothes, a microscope, and some botanical reference books which was obviously Jane's. Everything had been left as it was for the police to examine. Jane's passport was in the bedside drawer and with it her open-date return booking on the cross-Channel ferry, which had on it the registration number of her car.

Wondering why Jean-Louis had not bothered to find it and pass it on to the police, she made a note of it and prepared to go downstairs. But Jane's window was slightly open, and voices floating up from the terrace below sounded angry. To join the party on the terrace would be tactless. But she would not have been true to herself if she had failed to creep to the window and hear as much as she could.

The two men were attacking Adrienne.

'*Maman, tu divagues*,' said Jean-Louis wearily.

'*Oui, tu radotes*,' bellowed Emile.

Adrienne was defending herself indignantly against their suggestion that she was a drivelling dotard who had lost her marbles. What she had said was true, she insisted. They were all lying to her.

'Calm yourself, *Maman, chérie*,' Chantal pleaded. 'Why should we want to tell you lies?'

'You are mistaken,' said Jean-Louis sadly. 'You get confused, at your age it is to be expected.'

'I am not mistaken, I want to know. Why, suddenly, are you all in a new frenzy of quarrelling? Even the boring Greenwood noticed it and mentioned it in her letter to her mother.'

At this, mayhem broke out, with so many people talking at once that Celia had trouble following. Miss Greenwood got everything wrong, they insisted, there was no fresh quarrel. Were there not enough causes of disagreement already? Disjointed phrases floated up to the window. 'Not paying your share ... bleeding me white ... the poplar trees ... astronomical maintenance charges ... the park ... necessary repairs ... never paying your share ... farm labour costing us our eyeballs ... the poplar trees ... Philippe Dupont ... the poplar trees ... bleeding me white.'

Grievances going back to the beginning of time were being aired, and Celia began to make sense of them. In the settlement after Adrienne's husband died, the biggest farm had been Jean-Louis' share of the inheritance, and was his main source of income. Part of the deal had been that he should be responsible for keeping the park looking decent, and expect Chantal to pay her share of the cost. Chantal complained that she was paying for more than her share, to which he retorted that the work was done by farm hands on his payroll. But according to Chantal his calculations took no account of the fact that the hedges were cut by Philippe Dupont, who was on Adrienne's payroll, not his. Hortense kept repeating that the Marchants never paid their fair share of anything, to which Emile replied that the expenses of running the château were needlessly high and that every spare penny he had was needed to finance the expansion of his business. Meanwhile, Chantal continued to voice an obscure but bitterly felt grievance about poplar trees.

'You break my ear-drums with your poplar trees,' shouted Jean-Louis. 'When Papa died you gave us no peace till we agreed to put them in your share. Now, because the price has gone down, you want me to take them off you in exchange for something more valuable. There is no reason why I should, is it not so, *Maman*?'

'No,' said Adrienne. 'But there is also no reason why I should listen any more to this savagery. Go away, all of you. I shall not offer you an apéritif, you do not deserve it.'

Grumbling at Adrienne and each other, the two couples departed along the terrace to their own quarters. After a suitable interval Celia went downstairs, and out on to the terrace. Adrienne was still sitting there, recovering from her ordeal and fanning herself with a newspaper.

'*Ouf!* What a commotion!' she said. 'I hope the animal cries from my zoo did not inconvenience you?'

'You were the one who was inconvenienced, surely?'

'When I am having difficulties with my family, I often think of a saying by that charlatan Sartre. He said many

53

silly things but one sensible one: that "Hell is other people".'

'What particular brand of fire and brimstone were the family dishing out?'

'Oh, it was a silly affair. Since I came home two days ago, the air here has been thick with thunder. I was convinced that some new reason for attacking each other's throats had burst out while I was away. I wanted to find out what it was, because there are enough quarrels going on already without a new one. They said I was mistaken and I began to think that they were right, I was losing my brains, but when I saw those letters I knew that they were wrong. Just now I confronted them with what Greenwood had said, even she had noticed that there was a new quarrel. But they still denied it.' She paused. 'What have I done to deserve such children? How dare they tell me I am senile when all the time what I say is true? They are shooting each other down in flames in their quarrel, and when I tell them this is so, they call me a drivelling dotard.'

'How distressing. I'm so sorry.'

Adrienne gave her a woebegone look. 'Tell me, please, what I should do.'

'Have you no idea what they were quarrelling about?'

'None. Shall I send for them again and beat their heads till they tell me?'

Celia considered. 'This time the quarrel involves André and Anne-Marie as well as their parents. Am I right in thinking that they're both very fond of you?'

'I think so, yes.'

'Then perhaps they would tell you if you asked them.'

Adrienne brightened. 'My dear, you are right, you are much more clever than me in affronting this. They are nice children, they have not yet learnt to tell convincing lies.' She reached out a hand and gripped Celia's wrist. 'Thank you, my dear, for coming to give comfort to an old woman who is confused and sad because her family has no heart.'

54

Celia murmured something sympathetic, thinking it unkind to point out that this had not been her purpose in coming to France.

Antoinette was summoned. 'Go, please, and invite Mademoiselle Anne-Marie and Monsieur André to take an apéritif with us.'

'Wouldn't it be better to tackle them separately?' Celia put in.

'Again, you are right, my dear Celia. Antoinette, *n'invitez pas Monsieur André, seulement Mademoiselle Anne-Marie.*'

'*Bien, madame.*'

When she had gone Adrienne announced that there was no question of romance between the two cousins. 'They have known each other all their lives, as children they were put in the bath together, sex would discover nothing new. That silly sentimental Greenwood was imagining nonsense.'

'But they seem to be very close friends.'

'You see, they are allies in adversity, they dislike their parents as much as I do, and with much more reason. Chantal and Emile bully poor André without mercy, and Hortense tries to force Anne-Marie into becoming a vulgar snob like herself. But they revolt not only against their parents, they revolt against the whole bazaar, the rallyes and the snobbishness and the privilege and the anxiety to be exclusive. Hortense, who is ultra-snob, would like to force Anne-Marie into that world. Anne-Marie refuses and André supports her against her mother. This drives Hortense mad, but what does she expect? If young people do not become revolutionaries for a time, there is something wrong with them.'

Anne-Marie came into the room in jeans and a sweat-shirt and a jangle of barbaric earrings and brooches. With her grandmother's bright blue eyes, and her clear skin and dark curls, she was enchanting. Celia was not surprised that Jane Greenwood had drooled over her.

Adrienne told Antoinette to bring everyone a glass

55

of port, but Anne-Marie refused it. *'Pour moi un Coca, Antoinette, s'il te plaît.'*

When she had settled down with her Coca-cola Adrienne asked her what was new.

'Nothing that gives pleasure, *Grand-mère.*'

'But something that gives displeasure?'

Anne-Marie grimaced. 'Yes.'

'The quarrel which separates your parents from André's?'

'Yes.'

'I am very troubled, *ma petite chérie*, by all this brouhaha. What has happened to cause it? Tell me, please.'

Anne-Marie showed signs of distress. 'I am sorry, *Grand-mère*, I can't, because I don't know.'

'But surely, *chérie*? You have quarrelled with André, your great ally, because of it. You must know.'

'No, I have quarrelled with him because he will not tell me what the brouhaha is all about.'

'He won't, or he can't because he too doesn't know?'

'He knows. He says there is nothing new, it is just the old battles being fought again, but he is lying. Something has happened, and he knows what it is. He was there when they were yelling at each other like animals in an abattoir.' She collapsed into tears. 'For the first time ever, he allies himself with his terrible parents against me.'

Adrienne gathered her into her arms and murmured consolingly.

'I can't stay here,' Anne-Marie sobbed. 'All this shouting and anger frightens me, without André to support my morale it is intolerable, I shall become ill.'

'Calm yourself, my little angel. We will combine something so that you are not frightened.'

When she was a little more composed, Adrienne made a proposal. 'Listen, *ma chérie*. Suppose I telephone to your cousins in the Languedoc, and ask them to invite you.'

She raised her head, and considered this suggestion.

'But nothing ever happens there, except endless games of tennis. *Là au Languedoc, c'est pas du gâteau.*'

'*Pas du gâteau?*' Celia echoed, amused.

'That means "it's tough",' Adrienne explained. 'It's slang, but there's a song about it that Anne-Marie and André sing sometimes. Sing it to us, Anne-Marie my dear.'

'But I haven't got my guitar. Besides, some of the words are rather rude.'

'Then tell us about it, *ma chérie.*'

'It's by a group called Les Inconnus,' Anne-Marie began. 'We got the words off the cassette. Their songs are always satirical, and this one is about the awful sufferings of the spoilt children of rich families, the sort you have to meet if you go to the rallyes. In the song they complain that they have to live in grand houses in chic parts of Paris where nothing vulgar like Arabs or supermarkets is allowed, and if they're too lazy or stupid to get into one of the Grandes Écoles, they'll have to resign themselves to being a director of father's firm. They live on caviare and salmon, and they had Ferraris even before they were old enough to drive them, and they complain that all this is quite sickening, so they have to revolt. And after each verse there's a chorus:

'*Auteuil, Neuilly, Passy, c'est pas du gâteau,*
Auteuil, Neuilly, Passy, tel est notre ghetto.'

'You see?' said Adrienne. 'Living in those chic places is not a gâteau, it's a miserable capitalist ghetto, and you have to reject it energetically. What do you decide, my dear Anne-Marie, about the Languedoc cousins?'

She made a face. 'Oh, *Grand-mère*! It's so boring there.'

'True,' said Adrienne. 'Last time I was there I almost dislocated my jaw with yawning. But you need not stay long, just till the fracas here has exhausted itself. If you went soon you could avoid having to attend Madame de Mirecourt's rallye.'

'So I could,' she said, brightening a little.

'So shall I arrange it?'

Anne-Marie hesitated before accepting the lesser of two evils. 'Yes, please, *Grand-mère. Maman* will be furious when I escape attending the *rallye*, but I must get away from this hell of quarrelling.'

'Leave dealing with Hortense to me, I will make myself your lightning conductor. And now, *chérie*, you must run along, it is time for all of us to have our dinner.'

When she had gone Adrienne gave a malicious little laugh. '*Pas du gâteau*. She and André sing that song under Hortense's window to annoy her. The silly sentimental Greenwood heard it and concluded that it was a gentle serenade which Hortense did not appreciate.'

Over dinner Celia suggested that André should be tackled next, but Adrienne thought for a moment, then said: 'No. I shall not send for him. If he lied to Anne-Marie, he would lie to me also. He would hate that and so would I. Already he is very unhappy.'

'His parents bully him, you say?'

'It is Chantal principally, she has this great hunger for money. She and Emile were living in Bordeaux before Edouard died, and his business was not at all successful. They came here when she inherited her share of the estate, which included numerous farms which are let to tenants. The rents are controlled by law and not very high, but a year ago one of the tenants died and Chantal decided to take the farm and exploit it herself, which would be more profitable. But the syndicate of peasant farmers, which is very powerful, said, "No, you cannot do that, you are over the age limit, when a farm falls vacant it must be taken by someone young, that is the rule." They thought, you see, that she would have to give it to one of them. But instead Chantal said, "Very well, if that's so my son who is just twenty-one will farm it." '

'And André agreed?'

'No. He has brains and wanted to study law, but Chantal gave him no choice. Everyone knows he has no training in agriculture, it is a fraud and a pretence which has made us very unpopular in the village.'

'Was that why that man shouted and spat at Chantal? Jane says he was a peasant.'

'She was right. It was no doubt Jean Sorel. It was he who tried to stop her plan for taking over the farm. He wanted it for himself.'

They ate for a time in silence. Then Adrienne said: 'What can it be that André would not tell Anne-Marie?'

'Something quite awful that his parents had done? So awful that he was ashamed to tell her?'

'No. He hates them. When there is something to their discredit, he tells her at once.'

'Even if it had to do with Jane Greenwood's disappearance?'

Adrienne looked startled. 'How could that be?'

'I have no idea. But could there be a connection between this great row and what happened to Jane?'

Adrienne thought for a long time. 'I don't see how. According to her letter she goes off into the Sologne to pursue her strange enthusiasm for moss. While she is there, something happens. How could anyone from Fleury be involved?'

'I agree. The Sologne is the place for the police to pick up the trail.'

'With the aid of the particulars in poor boring Greenwood's letter, the one which will tell them how to find the exact spot.'

'Yes. I'm sorry that it involves letting them see Jane's embarrassing observations about your unruly family. They won't take much notice of them, though, because it's clear that they're not relevant.'

Adrienne sighed. 'Even so, it is unfortunate.'

Next morning, refreshed with delicious coffee and rolls brought to her in her room by Antoinette, Celia set out to stimulate the criminal police in their search for Jane Greenwood. At the gendarmerie post in a neighbouring village she was told that the person to contact was Inspecteur Picot of the Police Judiciaire, who was to be found at the grandly named Hôtel de Police in Orleans. Given directions by the Adjudant in charge of the Gendarmerie, she found it in a side street some distance from the centre of town, a large modern building. The sight of its imposing bulk immediately set off the illogical fit of nerves which she always felt at the prospect of having dealings with the police.

Its small car park was full. But she found a place in the line of parked cars in the quiet street outside. A motorcyclist with a pillion passenger appeared from nowhere and came roaring down the street, so she waited for him to pass before crossing the road. But instead of passing by, the motorcyclist drew up beside her as if to say something.

But he did not speak. The pillion passenger had dismounted. They both had scarves over their faces and the visors of their helmets were pulled down. She was about to be mugged.

The police advice was, don't resist, give them the money and let them go. But before she could follow it, a violent push sent her sprawling, flat on her back. Above her, a booted foot was poised to stamp down on her face. She managed to roll aside, and the foot hammered down on her shoulder. Screaming with pain and fear, she managed to kick the man in the groin as he prepared to strike again.

Attracted by her screams, two policemen came running out of their headquarters. On seeing them the muggers remounted and shot off down the street, taking with them her handbag.

The policemen picked her up, handed her her car keys which lay on the pavement beside her, and took her into the building to recover and make a statement. Nursing her aching shoulder, she reported the loss of her make-up, a largish sum in francs, and her visa card. As she was describing her assailants, a fattish motorcyclist and a smaller, thin pillion passenger, realization hit her: Jane's letters had been in her handbag too.

When she mentioned this, and explained why she had brought them, she was given a glass of water and a hard plastic chair to sit on while Inspector Picot, the detective in charge of the case, was found.

The loss of Jane's letters was worrying. She could describe their contents, but would she be believed by this unknown Inspector? Would she be suspected of double dealing of some kind? Her morale, already badly shaken by her mugging, sank even lower. She had had too many unpleasant experiences in the past, being shouted at by policemen who did not believe what she was saying. French policemen would probably be experts at smooth sarcasm, rather than loud-voiced bully-boys.

Getting more apprehensive every moment, she was collected by a policewoman and ushered into an airy office on the third floor. It contained a large young man with dark hair and pleasantly open features, very clean looking and well built.

'Inspector Picot?'

'*Oui, Madame, c'est moi.*'

He could hardly be out of his twenties. In slacks and an open-necked shirt, he was a welcome substitute for the grim-faced older man whom her forebodings had led her to expect.

'Concerning the affair of Mademoiselle Greenwood, Madame, is it not?' He produced a file from his desk drawer and opened it. 'Ah, yes. She was staying at the Château de Fleury near Beaugency, but last Sunday she drove away in her car, leaving her passport and personal effects in her room, as if she expected to return.'

'That is correct,' said Celia.

'And when she did not reappear, Monsieur Jean-Louis de Fleury alerted the local gendarmerie, who made the normal enquiries. If she had been injured or killed in a traffic accident it would explain her failure to return, but no accident involving a person of her description has been reported and enquiries about hospital admissions also proved negative. For these reasons the disappearance of this lady is being treated as a criminal matter. May I ask, Madame, why you are concerning yourself?'

Celia explained that she was a friend of the family. It was important to find Miss Greenwood because her mother was gravely ill. She had come because she had information which she believed might be of use to the police. It was contained in Jane's letters to her mother. Unfortunately they had been stolen from her handbag by muggers.

He frowned. 'There is a drug problem here. Muggers are very active in the city centre. Did these letters throw light on the reasons for her disappearance?'

'I'm sorry, no. But Miss Greenwood was a botanist, who disappeared while on an expedition to collect specimens in the Sologne. I was going to give them to you because details in them make it possible to identify a spot which she visited on the day she disappeared.'

'But you have read these letters, Madame?'

'Of course. Very carefully.'

'And I hope you have a good memory, and can tell us the details which will help us to find this place. I will fetch a map, and we will look at it together.'

He went, but a remark of his had started an alarming chain of thought. According to him muggers were active in the city centre, but what were they doing in a quiet suburban street, right outside police headquarters? Were they really drug addicts desperate for a fix?

Or had her bag been stolen because it contained the letters? Surely not, there was nothing incriminating in them, no clue suggesting a motive for harming Jane Greenwood.

Had someone from Fleury stolen them to prevent the family's dirty linen being displayed to the Police Judiciaire? It was a prospect they all hated, but would they have resorted to violent crime to stop it? No, on second thoughts that idea was nonsense. There had been two motorcycling muggers. The pillion passenger was slightly built and could even have been a tallish woman, though his companion, much more heavily built, was almost certainly a man. What possible pair of allies from Fleury could be responsible? Jean-Louis and Emile? Out of the question, they were at daggers drawn. Jean-Louis riding behind fat Hortense? The imagination boggled. Fat Emile and Chantal? Just as unlikely. No, this was a routine mugging by junkies out for money. She was small and white haired, it had happened because she looked like a soft target as they rode by.

Picot came back with a large-scale map. 'Show me now please where I am to find this place which is mentioned in the letters.'

She found the spot at once. The pool was clearly marked, on the corner of the drive leading to the Château des Étangs. 'It's there, Inspector.'

'You're sure, Madame?'

'Absolutely.'

He was looking suspicious. 'The details in the letter must have been very precise.'

'Actually, I've been there,' she confessed. 'There are footprints which I think must be Jane's in the mud at the edge of the pool.'

'You went there? Why?'

'Let us say curiosity, Monsieur. And anxiety for Miss Greenwood. I hope you don't mind.'

Celia quailed under his disapproval. His shrug suggested that nothing better was to be expected of an eccentric Englishwoman. But he listened attentively as she described Jane's meeting with the man with the gun, and her own conversation with him.

'His name, Madame?'

'Etienne Lamotte.'

He made a note. 'I shall speak to him. You do not know the *immatriculation* of Mademoiselle Greenwood's car?'

'Oh dear, I made a note of the number, but it was in my bag. It began with the letter C, that's all I remember.'

'Would you recognize it if you saw it?'

'Probably, yes.'

He wrote a number on a slip of paper and handed it to her.

'That's right!' she said. 'I'm quite sure. You've found her car?'

'It is here in Orleans, in the underground car park by the cathedral. Our attention had been drawn to it because of the length of time it had been there, causing the parking charges to mount up alarmingly.'

'So whatever happened to her took place here, after she'd parked the car.'

He looked solemn. 'We do not know that she drove the car from the Sologne herself.'

A chill struck Celia. 'You're suggesting that someone else did? Someone who had killed her?'

'Unfortunately it is a possibility.'

'But she wasn't . . . killed there by the pool. I saw no sign of a struggle.'

'She could have penetrated further in the wood, Madame.'

'But Etienne Lamotte told her not to. She mentioned that in her letter.'

'Is she a person who would be likely to ignore such warnings?'

'I didn't know her well,' Celia confessed. 'But . . . yes, I think she might go exploring if she saw something of botanical interest to her. Even so, what could have happened to her?'

He shrugged. 'An encounter with some violent person, a poacher perhaps. Even a gamekeeper, some of them have very easy triggers.'

'Surely not,' said Celia, her Scots blood appalled by the idea of a trigger-happy gamekeeper.

'These are only possibilities, I do not wish to distress you. But large parts of the Sologne have been bought up over the years by rich people from Paris, which is only two hours away on the autoroute, who come at weekends in winter for the shooting. The gamekeepers spend the whole year rearing birds for the Parisians to kill, and they know that their jobs will not be safe if the scale of the slaughter is judged to be insufficient. If they see something move indistinctly in the undergrowth they assume it is a poacher. They fire first and ask questions afterwards.'

'*Quelle horreur*, what a shocking idea. Monsieur Lamotte seemed a very pleasant man, and he was quite relaxed when he talked to me.'

Picot smiled. 'I probably do him an injustice, because I am prejudiced against the Parisians and their employees. I myself am from the Sologne, and I resent very much what they have done to the region, putting house prices out of the reach of the local people and enclosing so much land that to go out with a gun is no longer a pleasure.'

Celia reflected that a policeman with a down on Parisians might well have similar feelings about people who lived in châteaux. It was fortunate, she decided, that he would not be poring over Jane Greenwood's observations about the quarrelling family at Fleury.

'You are quite certain,' he added, 'that Mademoiselle Greenwood's letters contained no clue which would help us in our inquiries?'

'I've thought very hard about this. There was a lot in them about her research into mosses, which was what took her to the Sologne. Otherwise they were about her work for Madame de Fleury, preparing her son's botanical drawings for publication, and the difficulties she was having because of differences between French and British practice. She consulted someone at the university here about that.'

'Do you know who?' he asked, making a note.

'She didn't give a name, but she thought he was the Professor of Botany. Her letters also described life at the château, which was of course a novelty to her.' She paused, wondering whether to mention the Fleury family's inbuilt tendency to quarrel. Conscience told her that she must. 'There was a certain amount of tension between members of the family, and she remarked on that.'

She waited, expecting to be asked for details. Surprisingly, she was not. After a short pause, Picot said again: 'You are quite sure, Madame, that the letters contained nothing which might be useful?'

'Quite sure. I'm sorry.'

65

'So you can help us no more?'

It was her turn to hesitate. Were the people who had snatched her bag ordinary muggers? What other credible explanation was there? It was inconceivable that anyone from Fleury could be involved. But why had it happened in a quiet street, right outside police headquarters?

If he thought she had been mugged down in the city centre, he was wrong. She should have mentioned that right at the beginning. If she pointed it out now, he would think she was implying something sinister, and ask for explanations which she could not provide. The uniformed policemen she had dealt with downstairs would probably put him right anyway.

'I'm afraid that's all I can tell you,' she said, and rose to go.

FOUR

Inspector Picot turned off the road into the sandy track leading to the Château des Étangs and the pool where Miss Greenwood had gathered her specimens. He knew the area well. The track led to an open space which acted as an informal parking place, for it was the starting point of the middle section of one of the long-distance trails through the Sologne, signposted for hikers with coloured marks on trees.

Just past Miss Greenwood's pool, which was dimly visible through the trees, he turned off the track into the drive and up to the château, which he eyed with distaste. By his reckoning it was the sort of building that a Parisian *nouveau riche* who had made his pile would have put up a hundred years ago to mark the fact that he had risen in the world, and could afford to pretend to be a country gentleman, if only at weekends. It had probably changed hands several times since, but only between unpleasant townee 'sportsmen' from the same social bracket as its original owner.

On the other hand, he found Etienne Lamotte hard to dislike. He was obviously a local man with a feeling for the countryside. His account of his dealings with the missing lady was laced with humour at the expense of her eccentricity, but not really unkind. Yes, he had seen her on the Sunday, when he drove out to attend the eleven o'clock mass at La Ferté. When he came back, she and her car had gone.

'And that was when, exactly?'

67

'After mass I had a drink in the little bar by the church, but I must have been back here by half-past twelve. On Sundays in summer all sorts of strange people come along this track. Not just thieves, but people who crash about in the woods and disturb the pheasants. I don't like to leave the place empty for long.'

'Good. Now, in a few minutes a dozen men from the gendarmerie mobile will be arriving to search the woods near where she was last seen—'

He looked alarmed. 'But her car had gone. She had driven it away.'

'Someone had driven it away,' Picot corrected. 'And as you say, on a Sunday in summer there are all sorts of strange people about. I believe you warned the lady not to penetrate further into the woods?'

'I made gestures. It was all I could do, because she spoke no French. But I think she understood.'

'It is possible that she did not, or she may have ignored your advice.' Picot paused significantly. 'I don't want to make needless trouble for you, but also, I don't want to have to summon ambulances for gendarmes injured in fox-traps. So if there's anything embarrassing of that kind hidden in the undergrowth, I suggest you remove it before they arrive, and I'll shut my eyes while you do it.'

Lamotte made a disgusted face. 'It's nice of you to offer, but the question doesn't arise. I'm not that sort of gamekeeper.'

'Good. I didn't think you were, but I decided I'd better say something, in case. Could you come and show me the pool where the lady was collecting her specimens?'

As Lamotte led him there he studied the sight lines. The patch of mud and moss could be clearly seen from the drive leading to the château, but not from the public track. All that a passer-by on it would see was that there was a pool, half hidden in the trees. The victim could have been killed beside it, and no one would have noticed anything amiss. But had she been killed there? Not while she was collecting her specimens, her footprints in the mud showed no sign of violent disturbance.

The minibus with the posse of gendarmes drew up at the side of the track. Picot's team-mate Michel Raynal was with them to guide them to the right spot.

Raynal was in his late twenties, a year or two older than Picot. The son of a small shopkeeper in the outskirts of Orleans, he came from the same underprivileged background. As an Enquêteur Première Classe he was inferior to Picot, who was an Inspecteur, but they were good friends as well as effective working partners. Picot had the theories, Raynal raised the objections. Picot supplied the drive and energy. Raynal, more down to earth, tied up the loose ends.

'*Hé*, Jacques, what goes on?' Raynal asked, descending from the minibus.

'Come over here and I'll show you.' Picot took him over to the pool. 'See those footprints? This is where she was last seen.'

'What was she doing, trampling about in the mud?'

'Gathering moss.'

'She was *dingue*, then?'

'No, Michel. A perfectly sane botanist, but with a strange speciality.'

'If you call that sane,' Raynal grumbled, and transferred his attention to the pool. 'Do we have to drag it?'

'Let's stay dry till the wood's been searched. We'll do a sweep this side of the pool first, then the other side. If there's nothing, we'll have to search right through the wood.'

'It's big. Are you sure she's here?'

Picot made a face. 'For all I know, she may have parked her car in Orleans and thrown herself into the Loire.'

'Don't tell the troops that, it'll discourage them.'

They disembarked the men, and formed them into a long line. They advanced, shoulder to shoulder, probing the undergrowth. The area near the pool yielded nothing. Urged on by Picot and Raynal, the line pressed on into the depths of the wood. It was slow work. Every clump of entangled undergrowth had to be thoroughly probed.

'At this rate we'll be here for a week,' grumbled Raynal.

But far away in to the left of the line someone was shouting. Something had been found.

Raynal hurried over to investigate. Picot followed grimly, without hurrying. He was used to murder cases by now, but he still needed to steel himself against the first shock.

Raynal pointed to what looked like a random pile of brushwood. 'In there.'

The murderer had been in too much of a panic, or too much of a hurry, to bury his victim. But he had dumped her in a thick patch of undergrowth and collected fallen branches to pile on top of her so that she was almost completely hidden. She would not have been found for days, perhaps weeks, if her letter to her mother had not told the searchers where to look.

All Picot could see was a hand and part of a bare arm. When he shifted the covering branches a little to get a better view, he found that the corpse was naked. A sex killing, obviously. It looked as if she had been strangled.

He set the familiar routine in motion, sent for forensics and the police doctor. The gendarme began a minute search of the immediate surroundings for the victim's clothes, and anything else that might provide a clue. Picot and Raynal drew aside to confer.

'This sort of thing always sickens me,' said Picot. 'Some sex-obsessed joker with a kink raped and killed her.'

'So we pull in all the local ones we've got dossiers on, and check their alibis.'

'He may not be local. Her car was found parked in Orleans.'

'But he must have arrived on foot, if he drove her car away.'

'How about a gang rape, a collective of them?' Picot suggested. 'One of them drives away her car, while the others scarper in whatever jalopy they came in.'

'A gang high on drugs might batter the victim to death,'

Raynal observed. 'But she was strangled. Isn't that a bit too organized a method for gentry like that?'

'Right, we'll assume it's a solo job. We're looking for a randy type with perverted tastes who lives within, say, a twenty-kilometre radius.'

'Have to look them up in the files.'

'That's right, and find out what they were all doing last Sunday.'

Rather a boring job, Picot thought, involving a lot of leg work.

'Where does this track lead to, I wonder?' said Raynal.

Born only ten kilometres away, Picot knew. 'To a car park about a kilometre further on, where people leave their cars to join one of the long-distance walks. Its luck that she was killed on a Sunday, there'll be plenty of walkers about to act as witnesses.'

'Better call a press conference. Ask anyone who was here last Sunday to come forward if they saw anything unusual.'

'No, Michel. Not a press conference.'

'Why not?'

'They'd ask where our cadaver was staying before she became a cadaver.'

'Well?'

Picot looked grim. 'She was a guest at the Château de Fleury.'

Raynal was horrified '*Nom de Dieu!* Why didn't you discharge this bunch of thorns on to someone else?'

'Guercin's on leave and all the others were up to their heads in arson and drugs.'

'Who lives in this wretched château?'

'They're called de Fleury de Marcilly, and they've been there since the Middle Ages.'

'*Merde!* Not content with one *particule*, they have two. We are in the damn kneading trough once again, just our luck.'

They had reason to be worried. They had got into serious trouble two years ago, when they had worked

71

together on the case against Maurice de Bettencourt, a local bigwig with an aristocratic background and powerful connections in right-wing quarters in Paris. The evidence that he had murdered his wife was circumstantial, but there was a lot of it. Egged on by an examining magistrate with a left-wing background, Picot and Raynal had convinced themselves that he was guilty, and pursued him relentlessly amid a blaze of press speculation. Then fresh evidence appeared. It became clear that Madame de Bettencourt had been taking lovers promiscuously. One of them, the de Bettencourt chauffeur, had been jilted, and had killed her out of jealousy.

De Bettencourt's release and the arrest of his chauffeur was a development with exactly the right ideological overtones to produce an outcry in the right-wing press, to the effect that two inexperienced young members of the Police Judiciaire had been blinded by their ideological prejudices against people of birth and influence. Encouraged by an examining magistrate of similar views, they had spent months hounding a distinguished public man, while ignoring the real but proletarian culprit who had been under their left-wing noses all the time.

They had been misled and made suspicious of de Bettencourt by the number of lies that he had told to protect the posthumous reputation of his erring wife. But it was no use pleading that in mitigation, the right-wing papers had got the bit between their teeth and gone in hot pursuit of the wicked left. The examining magistrate, as the person officially in charge of the investigation, was transferred elsewhere in disgrace, and the two detectives received reprimands which threatened to affect their promotion prospects. If they got involved with another aristocratic family the hue and cry in the press would start up again.

'*Merde alors!*' moaned Picot, appalled.

'But, Jacques, it is not a comparable situation. She was killed by a sex-obsessed maniac twenty kilometres from the château. No one there is involved.'

'Such a detail will not be an obstacle for journalists of that political orientation. They will follow us when we go to Fleury, and wait for us to spit like savages on this noble family. When we don't spit, they will say we did.'

'Nevertheless we must go there,' Picot pointed out. 'Greenwood's clothes and effects are in her room. We must examine them.'

'We shall be walking on eggshells,' said Raynal gloomily.

The forensic officer, a woman, arrived. She took an extensive series of photographs of the corpse and its surroundings, then took charge of the victim's blouse, skirt, and underclothes, which the gendarmes combing the site for clues had retrieved from the rabbit-hole into which the murderer had stuffed them. The police doctor arrived soon afterwards, but refused to commit himself about the degree of sexual interference, if any; that would have to await the autopsy. He agreed that the cause of death was strangulation, but not with any of the clothes which had been recovered from the rabbit-hole. 'No, with something harder and less flexible.'

When the corpse had been despatched on its way to the mortuary at the hospital, Picot and Raynal prepared to leave. On reflection Picot had decided to send Raynal back to headquarters to extract the names of sexual deviants from the files, while he went to Fleury alone.

'How about informing the relatives?' Raynal asked.

'They're in England. I don't know who they are. But there's this Madame Grant, a friend of Greenwood's who seems to be representing the interests of the family. She's staying at the Château de Fleury. I can tell her.'

'Is she also obsessed with collecting moss?'

'I don't think so, but she puzzles me. Very small and svelte, with white hair, very composed in her manner. She came here herself and inspected the pool before she went into Orleans to alert me.'

'Strange. Why did she do that?'

'Heaven knows, but when she came to see me I had

the feeling that she was holding something back.'

'Holding back what?' asked Raynal, alarmed.

'No idea, but she was uneasy when she told me about Greenwood's letters to her mother being stolen by one of the motorcycling gangs. Among the crowds in the city centre, such a thing is common, but it happened right outside the commissariat, as she was on the way in. I found that out later, from Lemâitre down on the reception desk. Why didn't she mention it?'

'Perhaps she thought it unimportant.'

'Wouldn't she have realized that such things don't often happen in a quiet street in an inner suburb? No, I'm sure she had something on her mind. I think she suspected the motorcyclists of stealing the letters because there was something incriminating in them that they didn't want us to see.'

'If she thought that, why didn't she say so? Anyway, she insists that the letters contained nothing incriminating.'

'But if anyone had reason to fear what was in the letters, and knew that she was bringing them to us, they'd attack her outside the commissariat.'

'You're talking about someone from the Château de Fleury!'

'Not necessarily.'

'Who else? Jacques, you frighten me. Take care, or you'll have the Procureur after us with his thought police. We can't afford to think things like that about château-people with one *particule*, let alone two.'

'Don't worry. I'll behave like a well-trained little altar boy when I get there.'

But when he drove up the lime avenue and into the courtyard at Fleury, he had to take a tight grip on himself. Unlike Raynal, he had a chip on his shoulder and knew it. What got under his wick was not privilege of birth or position. It was the fact that privileged people tended to patronize him as a common, jumped-up policeman. He would have resented it less, perhaps, if he had not been born into a peasant family of tenant farmers in the Sologne.

The painted ceiling of the grand entrance hall reeked of aristocratic arrogance, but also of lack of funds to repair the cracks in the plaster. He tried not to resent the faded elegance of the salon into which he was shown by the servant who answered the door. But the elderly lady with very blue eyes, who identified herself on entering the room as Adrienne de Fleury, held out her hand to him with an arching gesture which implied that he could kiss it if he wanted. To do so would have been against his principles, but to be offered a hand at that angle by this sort of person was something. For once, he was not being patronized.

'You have met Mrs Grant, I believe,' she said as the silver-haired little Englishwoman joined them and extended her hand in a friendly but unkissable position. Picot's doubts about her rose to the surface, but he repressed them.

'You have news for us, Monsieur?' asked Madame de Fleury.

'Bad news, regrettably.' He believed in getting it over in one. 'Mademoiselle Greenwood has been found, dead. In a wood. Strangled. By a rapist, we think.'

Of the reactions, the Englishwoman's was the less violent. She nodded grimly, as if this was no worse than she expected. But the old lady took it very hard. Her face was ashen. She had been born into a world where such things did not happen, and even rapists knew their place.

But as he explained the circumstances she took a grip on herself. 'How disgusting. Poor Miss Greenwood, she was a fool and a bore, but she didn't deserve this.'

Picot addressed himself next to the Englishwoman. 'I regret, Madame, that I must ask you to perform the painful duty of identifying the victim.'

'Oh. I'm sorry, but I'm not the right person to make a formal identification. I've only met her once, at a conference three months ago.'

Curiouser and curiouser, he thought when she had explained the complicated course of events which had brought her to Fleury as the representative of the family.

75

Could her story be checked? He would have to think about that later.

'Some relative, perhaps?' he suggested.

The Englishwoman shrugged. 'The only relative I know of is her mother, who is bedridden with a stroke.'

He was dismayed. Space in the mortuary at the hospital was limited. He had no wish to have the corpse cluttering it up till some more mobile relative could be found and brought over from England.

'Miss Greenwood has been my house guest for the past month,' said Madame de Fleury. 'I would be prepared to identify her if that would be acceptable.'

'Thank you, yes,' said Picot, relieved. 'In conjunction with her passport that would be satisfactory. It is here, I believe?'

'In her room, Monsieur. Everything there has remained as she left it. Perhaps you would like to see?'

He accepted, and the servant was summoned to take him upstairs. Good relations with servants were often very useful, so on the way up he discovered that her name was Antoinette Dupont, and that her son Philippe was also in the family's service as an odd-job man and gardener. He also ascertained that two married children of Madame de Fleury's, a son and a daughter, lived in separate parts of the château. On the landing outside the bedroom he paused. 'You knew Mademoiselle Greenwood, Madame? What did you think of her?'

She shrugged. 'One cannot know a foreigner who understands no French, not a word.'

'But Madame de Fleury was on friendly terms with her?'

'No, Monsieur. She was not a person whom Madame would normally have admitted to her house. The English lady downstairs now, a very correct person, very amiable, she is a friend of Madame. With Mademoiselle Greenwood it was different. She was tolerated by Madame because she was here to work on the drawings of poor Monsieur Paul-Henri.'

She explained that they were botanical drawings, and that Paul-Henri, their creator, was a son of the house. But why was he 'poor'?

'He died, Monsieur, many years ago, in a terrible accident with his car.'

Dismissing her, Picot went into the bedroom. After a short search he found Miss Greenwood's passport in the bedside drawer, along with a car ferry booking form. A leather folder on the dressing-table contained a writing pad and envelopes, and also a number of handwritten letters in English. Taking possession of all these documents, he turned his attention to her other belongings and searched through garments and toiletries without discovering anything of significance.

When he went back downstairs he found the two ladies where he had left them in the salon, apparently still numb with shock. He handed the letters to the Englishwoman.

'These letters, Madame. Unfortunately I do not read English. I shall have to have them translated at the commissariat, but perhaps you can tell me what they are?'

Celia had read them the previous night, but had no intention of admitting the fact. Seized with guilty panic, she made a pretence of glancing at one or two. 'They are from Miss Greenwood's mother. The replies to the letters from Miss Greenwood which were stolen from me.'

What is she doing, this Englishwoman? Picot asked himself. She looked at them far too quickly; she did not need to examine them because she had read them already, I am sure of it. She goes to the scene of the crime before approaching me with her information, she has important evidence stolen from her, she gives the impression that she is holding something back, and now she reads the old lady's letters. Why? To assure herself that they contain nothing that she would prefer me not to see?

Had she abstracted any of them? And when she brought Miss Greenwood's letters to police headquarters, why had she not brought the mother's replies too?

In the context of a château and two *particules*, these

77

were forbidden thoughts. Picot choked them back firmly, and told Madame de Fleury how to get to the hospital mortuary in Orleans where she would find the body.

'Will it be convenient if I come this afternoon?'

'Certainly, Madame. The sooner the better.'

When he had gone Celia said: 'It was very noble of you to offer, Adrienne.'

'Oh, at my age one has seen death many times.'

But she was obviously shaken. Celia wondered if she was reliving the scene when she had to identify Paul-Henri, mangled in a horrendous car crash.

'Would you like me to come with you?' she asked.

'No, why? Philippe can drive me there. But a dreadful thought has struck me. What is to happen to poor Miss Greenwood when the police have finished dissecting her?'

'Horrors, I never thought of that. The police in Lewes are supposed to be finding some relative to come and sit by her mother's bedside. If they've found anyone, I can phone and ask what they want done.'

'You should warn them that the options are not numerous. I suppose she can't, even by stretching the imagination to its limits, be described as a Catholic?'

'No.'

'In that case she can't be put in the village graveyard here. It's reserved for the faithful.'

'Cremation, then?'

'No.'

'Why not?'

'There's nowhere to have it done. The church no longer insists that cremating people interferes with the resurrection of the body, but people still shrink from the idea.'

'Exporting a corpse to England is probably expensive too.'

'Oh, you will probably find a municipal cemetery somewhere that isn't too fussy about who it receives. Well, I suppose I should get her identified, if I can persuade Philippe to put on enough clothes to drive me there without outrage to morals.'

When she had gone, driven by Philippe in a smallish Renault, Celia applied herself to the cross-Channel telephone. There was little hope at this stage of getting a firm decision from the relatives, assuming any could be found, about funeral arrangements, but they had to be told, if possible, that Jane Greenwood was dead. Lewes police proved on enquiry to have ducked out of the chore of finding someone to come and sit by old Mrs Greenwood's bedside. They had wished it on to the social services, who passed Celia's enquiry from one extension to another till she lost patience. She would ring again in half an hour, she said. Would they please get their act together by then, and put her in touch with someone who knew what the position was.

Long before the half-hour was up, the telephone rang in its cubby-hole under the back stairs. On hearing Antoinette struggling with a caller who clearly spoke no French, she went to the rescue. 'Hullo, Celia Grant here.'

'Oh thank goodness, I couldn't understand a word that woman said.'

'Who is speaking, please?'

'I'm Winnie Appleton, poor Molly Greenwood's sister-in-law. That social service woman said you'd rung and gave me your number.'

She had been summoned, it appeared, from Leicestershire to provide bedside comfort for Mrs Greenwood, who was still 'very poorly, but getting better'. She was basing herself at the Greenwoods' cottage and going to the hospital every day by taxi, despite the horrifying expense. Her husband, back in Leicestershire, could not be left to his own devices much longer, he was 'helpless in the kitchen'. When was Jane coming back?

'I'm afraid she isn't, Mrs Appleton. She's dead.'

While Mrs Appleton made perfunctory enquiries about the manner of Jane's death, Celia could almost hear the brain at the other end ticking over. Who was to look after poor Molly when she came out of hospital? Surely one could not be expected to accommodate her in Leicestershire? She was showing signs of recovering from her stroke, and could not be relied on to solve the problem by dying. Meanwhile, how long was one expected to fork out for taxis and sit by the bedside?

'I was wondering about Jane's funeral arrangements,' said Celia. 'Would you be thinking of coming over to take charge?'

Cries of dismay greeted the suggestion of leaving the safety of England for terrifying foreign shores. 'Can't she be brought over here?'

'I'm afraid that would be expensive.'

More cries of dismay. 'Who's to pay for all this? Hubby and I can't, we've only got his pension.'

'Jane must have left a will. Perhaps you could look in her desk, and see what you can find out.'

'Oh, I wouldn't like to do that.'

Celia wondered if her husband, who might have a better business head, could join her and take a grip on the situation.

'Oh no, he's eighty and he's never been to London, even.'

Giving her up as a bad job, Celia rang her uncle Hugo's house. He was still away, but she made his housekeeper look up the telephone number of his solicitor, whom she rang with instructions to sort out the Greenwood finances. Sir Hugo had got her into this fix. He could damn well pay the solicitor's bill for getting her out of it.

She was feeling frustrated and restless. She could contribute nothing to the search for the man who had raped and murdered Jane, which was a matter for detailed police detective work and would probably take months. The only thing keeping her in France was the problem of how to dispose decently of the remains, and at whose expense. She ought to get back to Archerscroft. As in duty bound, she rang Bill, to warn him that her return would be delayed.

'Oh, Celia, how long for?'

'I don't know, Bill, I'm sorry.'

80

'Why? How come?'

'There's someone here I've got to get buried.'

'Buried?'

'That's right. You get a priest and someone digs a hole in the ground and you pop the corpse in.'

'Oh, a funeral! When's it fixed for?'

'It isn't. It can't be till the police finish their autopsy and release the body.'

'Oh, that sort of dead. Celia, you been at it again!'

'I know. I'm sorry, I didn't mean to.'

'You never do, but you're always off on some lark when you're wanted. Like you are now.'

'Why, what's happened?'

'Jenny Foster's been away all week with her stomach, and there's whitefly in number two glasshouse and them olearia cuttings is looking very miffy.'

'Oh dear, I knew we should have taken ripewood cuttings in the autumn. Have you ordered more *Encarsia* to deal with the whitefly?'

'Yes, but that's not all of it. Them squirrels from next door have been at the cyclamen corms again.'

'Shoot them.'

'I have.'

'Bill, it sounds as if you're managing wonderfully without me. Keep cheerful and I'll be back as soon as I can.'

Inwardly she felt horribly guilty about leaving him to cope, and cross with Jane Greenwood for delaying her return home. It was still very hot. Overtaken by a sudden desire for open air, she wandered out on to the terrace.

Anne-Marie was sitting on the grass by the round ornamental pool, staring into the water. On an impulse, Celia went down the steps and stood beside her. 'Hullo there.'

Anne-Marie looked up, a picture of tear-stained misery. '*Bonsoir, Madame.*'

'Oh dear, is the family quarrel still getting you down?'

'That, and also my mother is furious with me.'

'Because you'll be missing the *rallye*?'

'Yes, Madame.'

'I'm sorry.'

Silence. Anne-Marie was staring into the water again.

'And the Languedoc cousins don't seem to be much of an improvement on Fleury in its present state,' Celia ventured.

'No. *C'est pas du gâteau*, as they say in the song. I almost regret having agreed to go. To stay here and please *Maman* by going to the *rallye* would not have been much worse than going there and being bored.'

'And André is still being awkward?'

'Yes. While we could support each other and laugh about all these difficulties, it was tolerable. But now I don't know what to do.'

It was a cry from the heart, a state of mind that Celia recognized at once, having seen it before. Even the most strong-minded of teenagers had moments when they lost all confidence in their powers of decision and longed for a trusted adult to tell them firmly what to do. But what advice could she give this unhappy child?

'I am trapped wherever I go,' lamented Anne-Marie. 'Here, in the Languedoc, even in England.'

'Trapped?'

'Yes, Madame. Even in England one is imprisoned in a ghetto.'

'Oh, surely not. The English upper-classes don't build ghettos round themselves, they recruit pop-singers, entrepreneurs, anyone rich and successful into their circus. It can be quite amusing.'

Her face expressed disbelief. 'But I was in an exchange once with a Scottish family, very correct, very *rangée*, and it was just like here, except that shooting at animals and birds all day was substituted for tennis.'

Celia was fascinated. 'Where was this family?'

'Near Fort William, in the Highlands. Their name was Mackenzie.'

'Oh, but they're all cousins of mine, and you're quite right. They're dead boring, solid ivory from the neck up. But they aren't typical, you were just unlucky.'

'It was not bad luck, but the snobbish malevolence of my mother which put me there.'

'Look, when you're older you'll be able to escape from the ghetto. I did.'

'But how?'

'I married a fellow student who became quite an eminent horticultural specialist. You'll find university life quite liberating. But don't be disappointed if nothing much happens in your first year.'

'Nothing at all will happen,' said Anne-Marie despondently. 'When I go to the Sorbonne I shall be made to stay with my other grandmother, who is more snob than *Maman* even. Anyone who is not equipped with a *particule* will be chased away from me at once.'

Wrenching herself away from her contemplation of the water, she looked up at Celia with blank, unseeing eyes. 'I can find no future for myself, Madame. None at all.'

Celia was appalled. In all probability, this child was suicidal. She had seen blank eyes like that before, on the face of a girl who had hanged herself, a manic-depressive she had taken pity on and employed at Archerscroft. Something must be done, and quickly.

'Look, I have a suggestion,' she said. 'After my husband died I set up a horticultural business of my own. After you've done your stint with the Languedoc cousins you can come and stay with me if you like, and work in the nursery to earn some money for when you go to the Sorbonne.'

'*Ouais super!* May I really?'

'Of course.'

'And even *Maman* will be pleased, she says you are very correct, very *bon genre*, like those awful people in Scotland. But you are not like them at all. I shall give you a kiss, Madame, may I?'

'Yes, but do stop calling me Madame, my name's Celia.'

But before the kiss could materialize, Anne-Marie stiffened in alarm. She was looking over Celia's shoulder at someone approaching them from the house. Celia turned, and saw Hortense coming ponderously down the steps from the terrace.

'Anne-Marie, your dress has arrived. Come, please, and try it on.'

'What dress, *Maman*?'

Hortense raised her eyes to heaven in protest against such stupidity. 'The white dress that you are to wear at Madame de Mirecourt's *rallye*.'

'But I have told you, *Maman*. I shall not rig myself out in that silly white dress, I shall not let myself be dragged to Madame de Mirecourt's. I cannot go, because I shall be staying with the Languedoc cousins.'

'No and no and no, you will not, *petite idiote*! This talk of the Languedoc is some foolishness of your grand-mother's. She spoils you, and does whatever you want, because you run to her with sly little lying stories to please her, things that make me a monster and you a little martyred *sainte-nitouche*.'

'What I tell her is not lies, though your behaviour is so grotesque that it is often unbelievable. When she asks me why you and Papa are screaming like wild animals at my uncle and aunt, and I say I don't know, that is not lying.'

'We are not screaming at each other, this great new quarrel exists only in her mind, you tell her what she wants to hear. Age is softening her brain, she does not know what she is saying.'

'At least she manages to talk to me without bellowing like a discordant Valkyrie.'

'Anne-Marie, you will apologize at once for that remark.'

'I am sorry, *Maman*. I should have said like a Valkyrie who sings perfectly in tune.'

Hortense treated Celia to a martyred look, as if to say: 'What is a poor mother to do with an impossibly difficult daughter like this?'

Short of telling her to treat the child as a human being, there was no obvious answer. And it was now clear to Celia that Anne-Marie, far from being suicidal, was perfectly in control and able to defend herself. She withdrew into the house, then felt two strong complementary urges: she wanted a large whisky, and she wanted to get away from Fleury and its stresses for an hour or two. But where should she go? Somewhere on the banks of the Loire, perhaps. She would swig whisky in a café and watch the river go by.

She went to her car, which was parked in the covered arcade beside the courtyard, and sat in it studying the map. The choice of where to go was not easy. Most of the villages on either bank were a good way from the river, and Beaugency and Meung, which had river frontages, were quite large towns.

She had reached no conclusion when a car drove into the parking arcade, a little way along. Emile Marchant, back from his day's work, got out. But instead of locking the car and going into the house, he stood by it, as if waiting for something.

To judge from his expression as he looked out over the courtyard, what he was waiting for was about to happen. Celia squirmed round in her seat to get a better view, and saw Jean-Louis cross to where Emile was standing beside his car. Were they about to re-start hostilities? No, to her amazement he gave Emile a friendly clap on the shoulder and what looked like a conspiratorial grin. Then he fished out something he had been hiding inside his jacket, a packet wrapped in cloth, and handed it over with a smile. Emile put it in his briefcase. No word was spoken, and Jean-Louis turned away.

At that point, Emile noticed Celia sitting in her car and pretending to be intensely interested in her map. After a moment of shock, he pulled himself together. '*Salaud!*' he shouted, shaking his fist dramatically at Jean-Louis' retreating back. 'You throw pennies out of the damn window, then expect me to pay up! Eighty thousand for repairing that footbridge in the park, ridiculous!'

Jean-Louis stopped in his tracks, turned and saw Celia. Realizing what was expected of him, he said peevishly:

'That eighty thousand included your share of last year's bill for fencing, which you failed to pay.' Then, switching himself into his angry screeching mode, he added, 'It's intolerable, this penny-gripping attitude of yours, it's enough to make one vomit.'

He walked back to where Emile was standing, and they began to stage a furious argument about money. Celia had no doubt that it was a cross-talk act put on for her benefit. They suspected that she had seen their friendly little exchange, and were trying to obliterate the impression, convince her that they were still enemies. Why? Because if she found out that they had become allies, she might start to have a disastrous train of thought. But it was too late, the disastrous train of thought had already led her to its conclusion. She knew now that Jean-Louis and Emile were the two motorcyclists who had stolen Jane's letters outside the Hôtel de Police in Orleans.

While she digested this startling piece of knowledge, the two men went on shadow-boxing till they felt they had done it for long enough to fool her, then separated. Jean-Louis went back into the château and Emile came across to where Celia was sitting in her car. 'Sorry about the row, Madame. It happens all too often in our family, unfortunately.'

'A divided inheritance always raises problems.'

'True. Going somewhere, were you?'

'I felt I needed a breath of air.'

'Oh, it's the same with me, after a day cooped up in that factory. When I come home, I always have a noggin on the terrace while Chantal cooks my dinner. Join me, why don't you? I'd be delighted.'

Wondering what was next on the agenda she accepted, hoping to be offered whisky and not some sweet, sticky apéritif. To her relief, the drinks tray set out on the terrace contained only glasses and a whisky decanter. Emile poured them both out large tots, and got straight down to business. 'My brother-in-law's as mean as hell, I hate him,' he complained, fixing his prominent eyes on her. 'Money, money, money, always trying to get some out of me, it makes me very angry.'

He went on to explain that the Fleurys were without a *sou* between them. It was the profit from his factory that kept the château going. But Jean-Louis, who ran the family finances, was bleeding him white.

Celia was puzzled. There was no conceivable reason why he and Emile would want to steal Jane's letters. It was quite obvious that they contained nothing incriminating. The idea of two respectable middle-aged men dressing up in motorcycling gear to steal them was too grotesque to be credible, bag-snatching by junkies was an everyday event. Had she imagined the friendly clap on the shoulder and the conspiratorial grin? No, unfortunately. She wished she had. She was incapable of seeing, hearing, and speaking no evil when evil lay under her nose. But where was the evil, and how many people did it involve?

On his second stiffish whisky, Emile warmed to his subject. He had been a fool to marry into the aristocracy. His mother-in-law had trapped him into it, because the family had to get its hands on money somehow. She had been all honey at first, with a lot of talk about how romantic the world of industry was, and how she admired successful businessmen. 'Then after she got me spliced to Chantal, hop! I was just a vulgar upstart, the lowest of the low. My only job in the family was to bankroll it.'

Presently he switched his attack to Hortense. 'Jean-Louis married her for money, did you know? But there turned out to be a lot less lolly than he'd thought, that's why he's always coming down on me. She's a common little piece really, but marrying into the aristocracy has made her a shocking snob, as far as she's concerned I'm just a low-class tradesman who has to keep the whole bazaar solvent by the sweat of his brow.'

Chantal joined them on the terrace. He beckoned her to a chair. His pale, bulging eyes stared at her intently.

'*Chérie*, I was telling Celia why I hate your brother's guts.'

There was a slight pause before Chantal turned to Celia. 'I hate him too. As a small boy he was intolerable. As a man, he is *infect*, a *crapule*.'

But Celia had seen what went on during the pause. A look of astonishment, followed by the realization of what was expected of her, and then the response. There was a conspiracy, and Chantal was in it too.

How many of them were involved? Not Adrienne, Jean-Louis and the Marchants seemed to be ganging up against her. Hortense? Probably not, she seemed to be a figure of fun and an outsider. But what did the conspiracy consist of? Jane had been killed miles away in the Sologne, apparently by a rapist. If there was a connection with Fleury, what was it? Celia's mind was in turmoil. The only certainty was the fact that Emile Marchant and Jean-Louis de Fleury were secret allies, and had gone in for a lot of play-acting to persuade her that they were still bitter enemies.

Presumably Chantal's arrival meant that the Marchants' dinner was ready. She rose to leave, feeling depressed as well as confused. She could foresee that a moment would come when the laws of hospitality would count for nothing and her behaviour as a guest at Fleury would become far from ladylike.

FIVE

Picot and Raynal had spent a busy morning in the Sologne. Of the seven men in the area with a police record for violent sex crimes, four proved to have alibis for the time of the murder. One of these was produced by a wife with a suspiciously ready tongue, whose only concern was to keep her errant husband out of jail and earning. But as he was a paedophile, he could not conceivably have been interested in Jane Greenwood, and Picot rebuked the detective concerned for troubling the good lady unnecessarily. So far, the other three men on the list of potential rapists had not been traced.

In appealing for witnesses to come forward, he had issued to the media the location and telephone number of an incident centre he had set up in the gendarmerie at La Ferté. But at this early stage there had been no need to mention that the victim had been a house guest at a château, so the media vultures who had hounded him and Raynal over the de Bettencourt affair had not yet seen reason to gather. When he left the incident centre to return to Orleans, the only reporters waiting to ask questions outside were the man from the local paper and the Orleans representative of the Agence France-Presse.

All morning, people who had passed the scene of the murder on their Sunday outing had been phoning in. There had been over a dozen sightings of the victim's battered little red car with its right-hand drive, enough to establish that it had been parked beside the track by ten to eleven, and was no longer there at twenty to twelve.

One of the callers claimed to have seen another car, parked a hundred metres further along the track at the relevant time. Picot, realizing how important this might prove to be, left Raynal in charge at the gendarmerie and went to interview the informant himself. He found a family of five, eager to tell him all. As they lived near by, they had walked up the track instead of getting out their car and driving up it to the car park before joining the long-distance trail. Picot's first concern was to establish the exact timing of their Sunday morning walk. After some debate between the parents and their teenage children, a consensus decision was reached. They must have passed the scene of the murder at about twenty past eleven; in other words after Etienne Lamotte had passed by on his way to mass and seen Jane Greenwood at work by the pool, but long before he returned home. Her car had been there when they went by, but they had neither seen nor heard anything suspicious. The other car had been there too, parked further along the track. Was it the murderer's car? If so, they must have passed by while he was still there, perhaps putting the dead woman in her hiding place deep in the wood.

Asked to describe the suspect car the parents were vague, but the children proved to have been much more observant. They were positive that it was an off-white four-door Renault 5. If it was the murderer's car, Picot reasoned, he would want to get it away from the scene as soon as possible to a place where it would not be conspicuous. He would then have to return, presumably on foot, to drive the victim's car away and abandon it in the car park in Orleans.

Getting the Renault away from the scene need not have taken him long. There was a perfect hiding place for it near at hand. On a Sunday, dozens of cars would have been parked at the end of the track by parties setting out to walk the trail. No one would take notice of it among them. Walking back to the victim's car would take the murderer fifteen minutes at most, and driving it into

Orleans to abandon it an hour, more or less, according to the traffic. But the return journey from Orleans to collect the Renault would have taken much longer. Unless he had an accomplice to give him a lift, he would have to rely on public transport, but that would take him only as far as La Ferté. Unless he was prepared to risk drawing attention to himself by taking a taxi or hitch-hiking, he would have to cover the six kilometres from La Ferté on foot. Say four hours at most for the whole operation. But the car would be perfectly safe where it was till late in the afternoon. It would only begin to be conspicuous if it was still there long after the last walkers had driven off home.

Picot's next step was to have another word with Etienne Lamotte, about whom of course he had made searching enquiries. He was a widower and a practising Catholic. None of his informants gave any hint of sexual irregularity, and it seemed that his only fault, if it was one, was a rough way with poachers among his pheasants.

'When you returned from La Ferté,' Picot asked him, 'did you notice a car parked further along the track from where the Englishwoman's had been?'

'No.'

'I am sorry, I formulated my question badly,' said Picot. 'Did you fail to notice whether it was there or not? Or did you take note of the fact that there was no car there?'

'There was no car in sight when I turned into the drive. If I had seen a car parked alongside our fence, I would have wanted to know why, and taken my precautions against a possible intruder.'

'And does the same apply earlier, when you drove out to go to mass?'

'Of course. At that time also there was no car there, only the Englishwoman's. I always look up and down the lane, for the same reason.'

These answers confirmed Picot in his suspicions. If the Renault had not been there when Lamotte drove out, and had gone by the time he returned home, its occupant must have been someone with only short-term business in the area. Perhaps he had hopped over the fence for a moment to answer a call of nature. He could have been a poacher. But it seemed equally probable that he was the murderer.

Back at the incident centre in La Ferté, Picot gave his team of detectives a fresh set of queries to put to the public. Had anyone else seen a whitish four-door Renault 5 parked a hundred metres beyond the entrance to the Château des Étangs on the Sunday morning? At what time? Would the owner of this car come forward, so that he could be eliminated from the murder inquiry? Did anyone remember seeing a similar car enter the parking place at the end of the track around midday? Late in the afternoon did anyone notice a solitary man walking up the track to the car park? Did anyone see him get into the Renault 5 and drive it away?

When Picot returned to headquarters in Orleans, a report was waiting for him on his desk. Jane Greenwood's car had been taken from the underground car park by the cathedral for forensic examination. The only fingerprints on it were the dead woman's, but it had also been driven by someone with larger hands than hers, wearing gloves. Some fibres had been found caught in the upholstery of the driver's seat, which was worn and cracked. They did not match the clothes she had been wearing when attacked, but might have come from other garments in her wardrobe. The glove locker had contained some indigestion tablets of English manufacture, and also some carefully sealed envelopes, each containing a minute fragment of vegetation. These had puzzled the investigators greatly, until they discovered on the back seat a thick book which proved to be a learned treatise in English on the identification of the infinitely numerous species of moss. Nothing else of any interest had been found. But the investigators wished to know how the car was to be disposed of. Presumably it and its contents were the property of the dead woman's heirs. But in their expert opinion it was in a state of terminal decay and only fit for decent burial in the scrapyard.

So far Maurice Durand, the pathologist in charge at the hospital, had not produced his report on the autopsy. It was time for Picot to report to higher authority on the progress of the case, so he drove round to the hospital to hurry Durand up. '*Hé*, Maurice. Haven't you got anything for me yet?'

Durand handed over a typed report. 'I'd just finished it.'

Picot began to read. The victim had not been strangled with her own tights, as commonly happened, but with some wider and less flexible ligature such as a man's belt.

'Unusual,' said the pathologist. 'They're normally in too much of a hurry to take off their belts.'

Picot read on. 'Maurice, what on earth does this mean?'

'What it says, my dear Jacques.'

'No doubt, but look at this. "Extensive bruising in and around the vagina," you say, "and a number of small lesions. But no trace of semen anywhere." What conclusions do you draw from all that?'

'He used a condom.'

'Surely that's unusual?'

'Yes. But in these days of Aids, not to speak of genetic fingerprinting, even rapists know they have to be careful.'

'Lubricated?'

'Yes.'

'How serious were the lesions?'

'Scratches, really, and quite small tears.'

'But you're saying that a man wearing a lubricated condom was able to inflict small wounds as well as the bruising?'

'It was a very violent attack.'

'In that case wouldn't the condom have broken under the strain?'

'Not necessarily. It might have done.'

'But no semen was found. You're sure, Maurice?'

'Quite sure.'

'And no condom was found near the body.'

'Not that I know of.'

Picot thought for a moment. 'Maurice, suppose you're not a rapist, but a murderer with quite a different motive on his mind. You decide to disguise your crime as the work of a rapist, acting on impulse after a chance encounter with a woman in a wood. You're in no mood for rape, and anyway you have to avoid giving a specimen which could be used for genetic fingerprinting. How would you go about it?'

They discussed the possibilities.

'And your findings would be consistent with something done along those lines?' Picot asked.

'Yes. But they're also consistent with the other thing.'

'There's nothing that worries you about writing it off as plain honest rape?'

'Those lesions do, a little. I've said so in the report.'

'Not very clearly.'

'I only report the facts. It's your job to develop the theories.'

Pocketing Durand's report, Picot drove to the Palais de Justice to report as in duty bound to the Procureur de la République. Having heard Picot's outline of the facts, he decided at once that this was a case for an 'Instruction contre X', a prosecution of an unknown person on a murder charge.

'Judge Vautrin will be seised of this matter,' said the Procureur. 'Please report to him at once.'

Picot had expected something like this. Vautrin, tall, grey-haired, and with an aquiline nose, was one of the senior Juges d'Instruction, and a martinet. He would keep Picot, who was now under his orders, on a tight rein. He had obviously been put in charge because no one wanted a repeat of the de Bettencourt case, which had left a black mark on the whole department's record.

Vautrin was in his office, and obviously expecting him. As soon as Picot had briefed him, Vautrin began to read the riot act. 'The deceased was a guest at the Château de Fleury, you say?'

'Yes, Monsieur le Juge.'

'We are in the presence of a random killing by a sexually perverted person, after a chance encounter in the Sologne. It is inconceivable that any member of the Fleury family could be involved, and you will confine your contacts with them to a minimum. You have informed them of the circumstances?'

'Yes, Monsieur le Juge.'

'Then there will be no occasion for your returning to the château in the foreseeable future.'

'With respect, Monsieur, one further visit will be necessary. Deceased's clothes and personal effects are still in her room. And fibres found in her car need to be checked against her clothing.'

'Very well, Inspector. But in view of past history I must remind you to be careful. You are fully justified in believing that ancient families of position and privilege have no more rights under the law than the humblest of their compatriots. But please make sure that your manner in dealing with such people does not over-emphasize this self-evident truth in a manner which gives offence.'

'Of course, Monsieur.'

'In any case, your efforts will be concentrated in the Sologne.'

'Yes. I have already set up an incident centre in La Ferté-Sainte-Aubin.'

'Good. What results have we so far?'

Picot handed him the pathologist's report. Vautrin read it carefully. 'He used a *préservatif*, I see.'

'Durand was not quite sure of that. You see his remark about the bruising and the small lesions. In conversation with me he said that a murderer prompted by a quite different motive might have been attempting to disguise his act as a sex killing.'

Vautrin made an impatient gesture of disgust. 'Why complicate things, Inspector? Everything points to a straightforward case of rape. You have been checking on known deviants in the area?'

Picot told him of results to date and investigations still in progress.

'Good. What will you do to cover the possibility of a first offender with no criminal dossier?'

'I shall not have my eyes in my pocket, Monsieur. But we may have to look further afield than the Sologne. A car, a Renault 5, was seen near the scene of the crime at the relevant time. The murderer may not have been local.'

'Or the presence of the car there at that time may have been a coincidence.'

'Perhaps, but there have been widespread appeals for the owner to come forward. No one has admitted parking there.'

'We will issue another appeal, in case he missed the first one. It is important to eliminate this car if possible.'

'Very well, Monsieur le Juge.'

Conferring afterwards with Raynal in a bar near the commissariat, Picot was enraged as well as gloomy. 'He says I'm to ignore the bruising and lesions and exclude all possibilities other than plain straight rape. And he wants us to issue another appeal for the driver of the Renault 5 to come forward.'

'But we've done that twice already.'

'Exactly. If you'd just committed murder, you wouldn't phone the flics and say, "It was me you're after, it was my car that those people saw parked at the scene of the crime." '

'You're sure it's the murderer's car?'

'No, Michel, but it's a strong possibility which we should examine.'

As usual in their partnership, Raynal cast himself in the role of devil's advocate. 'But it can't have been the rapist's car, can it? Imagine him driving along the track. He sees the Englishwoman's car. But he does not see her, for she is at work by the pool in the wood, which can't be seen from the track. He doesn't know who the car belongs to or how many people have got out of it, or where they are. Nevertheless, he stops and says to himself, "I will go into the wood hoping to find a woman by herself, in which case I will rape her." '

'Say she isn't hidden away in the wood. She's sitting in her car, eating her sandwiches.'

'It all happens on a public trackway?' Raynal objected. 'He drags her out of her car and rapes her, with people liable to come along at any instant? Anyway, why is she eating sandwiches? It's not lunch time. Jacques, what are you trying to prove?'

'At this stage, there is no question of proving anything. I am exploring a theory. It is possible that someone who is not a rapist had a motive for killing the Englishwoman. He followed her into the Sologne. On recognizing her car he decided that she must be near by, and went into the wood in search of her. He killed and undressed her, and produced misleading appearances of rape.'

'What motive do you attribute to your sexually uninterested murderer?'

'At present I have no idea.'

'Nevertheless, Jacques, you are thinking forbidden thoughts. You are pointing the finger at the Château de Fleury.'

'Not necessarily.'

'Look, Jacques. Where else are we to look for your sexually uninterested murderer? Greenwood speaks no French. She has been in France for barely a month. Who but the family at the château could have had sufficient dealings with her to have a motive for killing her?'

'There are times when one cannot avoid thinking forbidden thoughts.'

By now Raynal was thoroughly alarmed. 'Your reasoning is logical, I admit. But don't let's go down that road till we've eliminated the other possibilities.'

'What other possibilities are there?'

'Several. For instance: a rapist is out in his car on a Sunday morning when he sees a woman, an English-woman, driving along by herself. He says to himself, "That

97

would be nice," and follows her to the spot in the wood where she is found.'

'Then he is a rapist with a very long time fuse.'

'How so?'

'He sees her driving along in her car, but he doesn't follow her at once. When Etienne Lamotte drives off to go to mass, she's hard at work by her pool, but the rapist's car isn't parked near hers. It isn't seen there till half an hour later. He isn't following an urgent impulse, he's a scheming rapist who bides his time. And when he's finished he's got two cars to dispose of, his own Renault Five and the victim's car. How does he manage it without an accomplice?'

'Very well then,' Raynal argued, 'the Renault is a coincidence. The rapist arrives on foot. He rapes and kills Greenwood and drives her car away.'

'He's a cautious rapist, isn't he? He knows he must use a condom because of Aids and he knows he mustn't leave it lying about afterwards to provide a specimen for genetic fingerprinting.'

'Like the rest of us, he keeps up with the march of science.'

'Isn't that more like the behaviour of a calculating murderer who isn't a rapist? That way we can account for the lesions, which are difficult to accommodate in a normal scenario of rape.'

'So we are back at the Château de Fleury, Jacques, where we have no business to be.'

'Alas, yes.'

After a frustrated pause for thought, Raynal returned to the attack. 'I still think the Renault is a coincidence. How on earth could your motorized murderer dispose of two cars?'

'Easily, Michel. He parks his own car among the others in the clearing at the end of the track, then drives the Englishwoman's away.'

'He's taking an enormous risk,' Raynal objected. 'Suppose someone in the car park notes the *immatriculation* of the Renault? It can be traced. Or are you assuming false number plates?'

'No. That would not be necessary. The risk was not great.'

'How so?'

'The murderer had hidden the body in a place where it would not normally have been found for some time. By then no one would have remembered the description of his car, let alone the number. But fortune did not favour him. In a letter to her mother, the victim had described the place where she would be found. We were able to pick up his traces far more quickly than he expected.'

'Thanks to this Madame Grant who is a guest at Fleury,' said Raynal.

'Yes. But I had the impression that she was holding something back. Is there some English aspect to this affair that we know nothing of?'

'Jacques! She is *petite*, you said. You are not envisaging her in the role of strangler?'

Picot grinned. 'Don't torment yourself, I am not as mad as that. But before indicating to us where to look for the victim, she visited the spot herself, which is not normal. And the letter to the victim's mother, which contained the information, was never produced.'

'It was stolen from her, Jacques.'

'True. By those motorcyclists. But I ask myself, did they steal the letters because they knew that they contained something incriminating them?'

'If there was anything of the kind,' Raynal objected, 'why did the English lady not tell you what it was? She assured you that it contained nothing likely to help us.'

'Because she was holding something back.'

'Why would she hold back incriminating facts, when she took steps to ensure that the victim should be found?'

'I have no idea.'

'According to you,' remarked Raynal, sounding frustrated, 'these two motorcyclists stole the letters to keep from us evidence which would convict them of murder.

And you are saying the unthinkable; that these two murderers came from the château.'

'Well, Madame de Fleury has a son and a son-in-law living with her there.'

'Jacques! No, really, there are times when you exceed all the limits.'

'It was only an observation, Michel.'

'You are saying that two distinguished gentlemen, members of a family well supplied with *particules*, mounted a motorcycle to commit a theft in the centre of Orleans. No, it was a banal affair such as happens every day, the work of drug addicts in need of money for a fix.'

'I repeat, it was only an observation, but there is one more fact to consider. So far there is no report of the Englishwoman's visa card being used in shops, as was to be expected, in the hour or two after the theft when it would have been safe to do so.'

'Of course not. It was a woman's card. It could not have been used by a man.'

'Now, Michel, it is you who are being unreasonable. What male member of the drug culture is unable to find a female accomplice to use the card for him?'

Celia was sitting in the salon, reading *Le Figaro* while Adrienne had her siesta. The window was open to let in the breeze, and outside on the terrace someone at the far end had begun to sing in a rather harsh soprano, accompanying herself on a guitar. Anne-Marie, no doubt. It sounded like the song she and André used to perform under her mother's window to annoy her. But she was singing it alone. Since André's defection she had to.

When she came to the chorus a second voice, a man's, joined in:

> 'Auteuil, Neuilly, Passy, c'est pas du gâteau,
> Auteuil, Neuilly, Passy, tel est notre ghetto.'

Had she and André made up their quarrel? If so, good

luck to them. Celia stepped out on to the terrace and was displeased to see that the male singer was not André, but Antoinette's reprobate son Philippe.

Anne-Marie saw her looking out, and they both waved cheerfully. This was indeed raising the flag of revolt. From Hortense's point of view the song itself was an outrage. For Philippe to take part in its performance made the offence infinitely worse, and the reaction came swiftly. Hortense began bawling and screeching out of the window at them. They replied with laughter and rude two-fingered salutes. Celia felt she had been guilty of something like medical malpractice. Her morale-boosting cure for Anne-Marie's depression had been a massive overdose.

Events that afternoon produced even more disquieting evidence to the same effect. Shortly after three, Anne-Marie came out of Adrienne's boudoir looking red-faced and furious, and walked past Celia without a word.

Adrienne followed her out of the room and stood looking after her with an appalled expression. 'Oh my dear Celia, what do I do now? She has become insane.'

'Horrors, what's happened?'

'She refuses to go to the Languedoc cousins. No and no and no, she says. The château smells of drains and damp old churches and the tennis balls are last year's and the cousins are "ivory from the neck up". Where does she learn such barbaric expressions?'

'I have no idea,' said Celia untruthfully.

'I shall make her go, of course. She must, after I had begged for the invitation.'

'Did she give any reason?'

'She says she has changed her mind because if she goes she will miss that wretched *rallye*, and her mother is sticking poisoned knives into her because of that, and she can't stand it any more. She says she's so flattened that she'll stay here and go to the thing for the sake of peace and quiet. Hortense has also treated me to a very noisy five-act opera about my wicked action in arranging the

Languedoc invitation, so I know what poor Anne-Marie has been suffering.'

'Adrienne, d'you think that's the true reason?'

'Of course not, my dear Celia. When Hortense is being a Valkyrie, the sensible thing is to get as far away as possible. Besides, did you hear Anne-Marie's naughty singing just now on the terrace? Not at all the way to calm one's over-excited mother, and turning it into a love duet with Philippe made it worse.'

'Then what is the true reason?'

Adrienne shrugged. 'Who knows what happens in the brain of an eighteen-year-old girl?' She brooded for a moment. 'I have dark suspicions that this *volte-face* may be due to a machination of Philippe's.'

'Would you like me to try to find out? I had a long talk with her yesterday, I think she might confide in me.'

Adrienne considered this suggestion for quite a long time. 'I wonder. Don't you think being questioned would make her yet more obstinate?'

Down in the hall, the front door shut with a bang. Antoinette could be heard greeting someone who replied in an angry female bellow.

'Hortense,' whispered Adrienne, peering down the stair well. 'Prepare yourself for act six of the opera.'

As angry footsteps advanced up the staircase Celia retreated into the library. Through the shut door she could hear Hortense wading noisily into action out on the landing. 'What is this I hear from Anne-Marie? She says she wants to stay here, but you forbid it and say she must go to the cousins. How dare you interfere?'

Adrienne's answer was inaudible. But muffled cries of rage from the boudoir made it clear that the argument was continuing in there.

Celia was on far closer terms of friendship with Anne-Marie than Adrienne knew, and was fairly confident of getting the truth out of her. She stole downstairs in search of her and, not finding her on the terrace, she rang the doorbell at her parents' end of the house. Hortense's cook-housekeeper directed her to the kitchen, where she found Anne-Marie ironing clothes with vicious emphasis as she worked off her bad temper.

'So you've changed your mind about going to the Languedoc?'

'Yes,' said Anne-Marie fiercely.

'And Philippe has taken over from André as the big brother?'

She banged the iron down fiercely on a T-shirt. 'That's right.'

'Because André still won't tell you what the grand quarrel was about?'

'Correct. How can we be friends if he doesn't trust me?'

'Even though your father and Monsieur Marchant seem to have made it up, he's still keeping you in the dark?'

'Yes. As for making it up, they no longer scream at each other and break my ears. But they still circle round each other angrily and show their teeth, like dogs about to fight.'

So the pretence of hostility was being maintained, as far as Anne-Marie was concerned.

'Anyway, Philippe is the big brother now,' said Celia. 'D'you really like him, or is it a case of any port in a storm?'

'He's useful to me.'

'Good. I believe in persuading men to make themselves useful. In what way, though?'

The movements of the iron had stopped. 'You'll tell *Grand-mère*.'

Celia hesitated. 'Not if you'd rather I didn't.'

'Promise?'

'Very well, promise. How is Philippe going to be useful to you?'

'He is going to find out for me what the quarrel was about, and what it is that André will not tell me.'

'Can Philippe do that?'

'I think so. He has friends in the village, people who will tell him things.'

'Do the people in the village know?'

'Of course. They know everything. Three years ago an old woman was murdered for the sake of the money in her woollen stocking, and they all knew who had done it. But they did not tell the police, that is not their way. It is a very closed circuit, they prefer outsiders to know nothing. It is possible that they know perfectly well what my parents have quarrelled about with Uncle Emile and Aunt Chantal. But they wouldn't tell me, because I am not in the circuit. For Philippe it is different. He belongs partly with the village and partly with us.'

'But Anne-Marie, what is Philippe getting out of this?'

'Nothing. He has always wanted us to be friends, and now, because André is no longer my friend, it is easier for him.' She let out a brief giggle. 'He has promised to take me on Saturday to a very vulgar, very sweaty disco in Orleans.'

Celia's mental alarm signals began buzzing. 'Don't you think you should be a bit careful about this?'

'Careful? Why careful?'

'Philippe doesn't keep his distance like an ordinary servant. Could you handle it if he got too enterprising?'

Anne-Marie burst out laughing. 'Oh, how ridiculous. You said it yourself, he's my brother. Besides, he's not interested in women.'

'Horrors. You mean, he's *tapette*?'

'Not even that. The only person he's interested in is himself.'

Anne-Marie went on with her ironing. '*Grand-mère* is determined to send me to the Languedoc cousins, it will be as bad as Siberia. Can you not persuade her to spare me?'

'I'll try, but I'd better not say anything about Philippe and the sweaty disco.'

'Nor Philippe's enquiries in the village, if you please.'

'Very well, but I still think you need to watch Philippe. He has his own purposes in all this.'

'Of course, and so have I,' said Anne-Marie firmly.

'There are advantages for both of us, and it is perfectly fair.'

Not entirely reassured, Celia went to confront Adrienne, uncertain what line of advocacy, if any, to adopt. To her surprise she found her and Hortense sitting on the terrace, apparently the best of friends.

'Ah, Madame,' Hortense began as she joined them. 'Children are such a burden and a plague, are they not? One never knows what difficulty they will make next.'

'They usually turn out all right in the end,' said Celia mildly.

Hortense took issue with her at once, citing cases of children known to her who had not turned out well at all. A recital followed in which the dropping of aristocratic names was laced with horrifying details of drugs, unsuitable sexual arrangements, Aids, suicides, and left-wing politics among the young of the noble families concerned. 'But perhaps, Madame, you have no children and have been spared these horrors?'

Celia retorted that on the contrary, she had a daughter married to a diplomat and a son with a logging business in Canada. To judge from her expression, Hortense considered the diplomatic daughter OK, but the businessman son less so.

'Hortense and I are agreed,' said Adrienne in a voice of suppressed amusement, 'that Anne-Marie must go to the Languedoc cousins, whether she likes it or not.'

'Yes, my mother-in-law is quite right,' conceded Hortense warmly. 'It is a thousand pities that she should miss the social advantages of Madame de Mirecourt's *rallye*. Although she thinks nothing of them now, she will regret it later. However—' She broke off to heave a heavy sigh, 'I agree that at present the important thing is to separate her from that crapulous upstart Philippe.'

'I was a bit worried, I admit,' said Celia. 'But when I said so she just laughed, and said he was quite harmless. She even referred to him as her brother.'

Something was happening to Hortense. She had gone

105

very red in the face and her massive frame was shaken by what looked like a huge but silent hiccup. Muttering a word of excuse, she rose and hobbled away down the terrace to her own quarters.

'Poor Hortense,' murmured Adrienne, brimful of mischief. 'It upsets her to hear it mentioned.'

Celia looked bewildered.

'Hadn't you guessed?' said Adrienne. 'What you said is right. He is Anne-Marie's brother, or half-brother to be more precise.'

'But I thought—'

'Oh, of course. You were misled by that letter written by the stupid Greenwood, who got everything wrong. She thought my Edouard had fathered Philippe, but he was seventy when Philippe was born, it's ridiculous. The truth is quite different. Antoinette, you see, was one of the servants here, and a very pretty girl. My handsome Jean-Louis is much more wicked than he appears. He started his career of nasty tricks and fornications when he was fifteen.'

'Oh. Then Philippe really is her half-brother. Is he really as harmless as Anne-Marie says?'

'Where sex is concerned, yes.'

'You're sure?'

'Absolutely. You see, Philippe is not interested in sex. I think he is probably a virgin. Don't look so unbelieving, it's true. Dozens of women have made attempts, including some quite alluring and artful ones, but without success. Also, a homosexual friend of Jean-Louis also failed, despite great efforts. Philippe is one of those followers of Narcissus who have exercising machines in their room and weights to lift so that they can develop muscles like cantaloups and admire themselves and feel good. He even goes to Paris for competitions where they shave their chests and oil themselves so that they can exhibit to each other their torsos. I think he even doses himself with muscle-building medicines which have a bad effect on his capacity for romance. Perhaps he is dimly aware that

106

women have something interesting under their skirt, but I doubt it.'

'So it doesn't mean anything when he stands about in provocative attitudes with his shirt off?'

'It has a meaning,' said Adrienne, 'but not what you think. The attitudes are provocative because he is demonstrating to us that as a zoological specimen he is far superior to his father, whose physique is not so impressive. Antoinette came from healthy peasant stock. Philippe's strength comes from her.'

'And you didn't send Antoinette away when you found out about Jean-Louis' pecadillo?'

'Naturally we did. For the birth and for two years after that she was with her family in the Touraine. Then Edouard and I went to see her and found this beautiful little boy, so different from his naughty schoolboy father. We were both charmed by him, and Edouard could not resist the idea of bringing him and his mother back here. I was a bit reticent and foresaw trouble, but Edouard insisted.'

'So Philippe has always known who his father was.'

'No! We were very careful to keep it from him. But last autumn, unfortunately, Chantal had an extra-spiteful fit of rage against Jean-Louis because of some problem about her share of the local taxes. So she stood on the terrace shouting and screaming, and reproached him in turn with all the bad things he had done since he was a child, including his gift to Antoinette of her enormous muscular bastard. And Philippe, who was working in the garden, heard everything.'

'And that's when he started to be difficult?'

'Of course. He wants us to recognize him as one of the family and give him a share of the inheritance. Fortunately he has not yet consulted lawyers who could tell him how to press his claim. Instead, he thinks he can dominate Anne-Marie and attack us that way.'

'Which is why even Hortense agrees that she must be sent away. But that's only a temporary solution.'

107

'It will serve until her quarrel with André is over,' said Adrienne firmly. 'When that happens, Philippe's attractions will disappear.'

'Aren't you surprised that they're not reconciled already? Relations between the two sets of parents seem to have calmed down.'

'Have they? Perhaps they think they should put on a civilized performance to impress you.'

Celia thought, but did not say, that on one occasion at least Emile and Jean-Louis had tried to give a false impression of continued warfare.

'What does Antoinette think of the way Philippe carries on?' she asked. 'Does she support his claim against the family?'

'Ah. Antoinette, you see, is a doormat. All her life she has accepted without question or protest whatever was handed out to her, including the attentions of a fifteen-year-old boy. She is an admirable servant, and I think she likes me, but only because disliking me would be too much of an effort. If Philippe gains his point over the inheritance she will be quietly pleased, if he does not she will waste no time being distressed. Meanwhile, she contemplates Philippe's extravagances with the placidity of a cow.'

Hortense came hobbling along the terrace from her quarters at the far end, and plumped herself down in a chair. 'There! I gave that girl a good talking-to, told her I'd changed my mind and of course she had to go to the cousins after she'd been invited.'

'And how did Anne-Marie take it?' asked Adrienne.

'Oh, she knows she has to take her marching orders when I tell her I've made up my mind. She always goes very quiet when I'm firm with her. "Yes, *Maman*," she said, "of course, *Maman*", and she went up to her room. I shall put her on the morning train tomorrow.'

Pleased with herself, she stayed on, chatting and clearly delighted to find herself on reasonable terms with her mother-in-law for once. This sentiment did not seem to be echoed by Adrienne, whose expression combined quiet mockery with wonder about when Hortense would go. This did not happen till it was time for the two households to change for dinner.

'Hortense is a very stupid woman,' said Adrienne, looking after her as she retreated along the terrace. 'Even after all these years, she has not realized that when Anne-Marie goes very quiet it is not a good sign.'

Within five minutes Hortense was back, rushing along the terrace and uttering great gasps of alarm.

'What on earth's the matter?' asked Adrienne.

A few moments passed before Hortense became capable of coherent speech. It seemed that Anne-Marie, on going upstairs, had packed a bag. And according to Hortense's housekeeper, she and Philippe had just driven away in Adrienne's car.

SIX

It was Sunday evening, exactly a week after Jane Greenwood's murder. Picot and Raynal surveyed the company assembled in the clearing which served as a rough car park for hikers on the long-distance trail. They were well satisfied with the response to his appeal. Fifteen assorted cars had answered the invitation to take part in a police reconstruction. Only one of them was a Renault 5, and it was the wrong colour.

'*Bonsoir, mesdames et messieurs,*' said Picot when he had gathered the company round him. 'May I say first how grateful I am to you all for your co-operation. I have called you together because we are anxious to establish whether an off-white four-door Renault Five was parked here last Sunday. Does anyone remember seeing one? If so, perhaps you would raise your hand.'

No hands were raised. He tried again. 'We are anxious to eliminate this car from our enquiries. Does anyone know of a friend or neighbour owning one, who might have been here on that Sunday, but is not present this evening?'

Again there was no response. 'Let us make a great effort of memory. Would everyone please try to remember the colour and size of the vehicles parked on either side of them?'

A mass consultation followed, but all that emerged from it was a picture of the haphazard way the cars had been parked. The clearing had not been marked out with parking spaces, that would have been impossible on the sandy soil. People simply parked where they pleased, with the first comers taking the best places round the edge under the shade of the trees. They had arrived to find the centre of the clearing empty, but by mid-morning a straggling line of cars had begun to build up across it. By twelve, this line was complete. A young man with a crew cut and a louche-looking girlfriend who had arrived around that time volunteered that he had found no room in the line and had had trouble finding a place elsewhere where he would not be obstructing anyone's getaway. By then, therefore, the Renault must have been in the line of cars in the centre of the clearing, if it was there at all.

Picot asked everyone who had parked in the centre to come forward and tried, with Raynal's help, to make them reconstruct the line of cars. There were gaps, of course, because not everyone concerned had answered the summons. But several chains of three or four cars emerged, and a woman at the end of one of them thought she remembered a whitish car on the other side of her. Pressed further, she said she thought it was smallish, with four doors, but she had not noticed the make.

It was the right size for a Renault 5, which was encouraging, but the description was far too vague for certainty. There was an unfortunate gap on the other side of the dimly remembered whitish car, and nobody further along claimed to have noticed it. But a couple who had parked on that side of the crucial spot were murmuring about something, and presently approached Picot hesitantly.

'The Meuniers aren't here, Monsieur,' the husband ventured.

'No,' added the wife. 'They went to her mother's today, they may not be back.'

The Meuniers, it seemed, were friends of theirs, whom they had seen driving into the clearing shortly after they did.

'We thought we should mention it, Monsieur, because we think they parked a little way along from us and they may have noticed something.'

111

'A little way along from us' seemed to mean somewhere near where the off-white car was supposed to have been standing. Picot noted down the Meuniers' address, thanked them all for their co-operation, and dismissed them.

Edging along impatiently in the line of cars leaving the clearing, he and Raynal exchanged impressions. 'Nothing conclusive,' Raynal grumbled.

'It sounds as if the Meuniers were next to the whitish car. We may have better luck with them.'

'If they're back, Jacques, and if they noticed anything. It was a miracle that we ascertained as much as we did.'

The Meuniers' address was a neat chalet-bungalow in the outskirts of La Ferté. A large Citroën standing in its driveway gave evidence that they were back home. Picot rang, and found a couple and their three children about to sit down to dinner. Apologizing for the interruption, he explained his business and put his question.

'Let me see now,' said Meunier. 'I ought to remember because we arrived late and I had to squeeze into a very narrow space.'

'You're telling me!' his wife chimed in. 'I had all the trouble in the world getting the doors open enough for the children to get out.'

'On one side was a big *familiale*, dark blue, I think,' Meunier decided.

'And on the other, Monsieur?'

He half-closed his eyes. 'Something much smaller.'

'What colour?'

'White, or perhaps cream.'

'How many doors?'

'Four, Papa,' said the eldest child, a boy. 'It was a Renault Five, like Uncle's, the same colour.'

'He's right,' exclaimed Meunier. 'I remember thinking it couldn't be my brother's because he's away on holiday.'

Not for the first time, Picot blessed the powers of observation of small boys. None of them had noticed the number, that would have been too much to ask. He pressed them all hard to tell him anything unusual about the car, a bent wing, an added spotlight, a doll dangling on a string in the back window. To his disappointment nothing of the kind emerged. But when he tried to discover how long the Renault had been left in the clearing, he was in luck again. To avoid tiring her youngest child, Madame Meunier had turned back from the walk before the others. When she arrived back at the car, the space where the Renault had been was empty and the time, she thought, was about four o'clock.

'The times fit,' said Picot excitedly as they drove away. 'Let's say an hour for driving Greenwood's car into Orleans through the midday rush-hour traffic and parking it by the cathedral. Then he's got to get back to the clearing to collect the Renault. He wouldn't draw attention to himself by hiring a taxi, so unless he's got an accomplice to drive him, he'll have to use public transport to get to La Ferté; a bus along the Route Nationale or a train.'

'The train isn't direct,' said Raynal. 'He'd have to change at Les Aubrais.'

'Either way, he'd need at least an hour, which brings us to two o'clock.'

'Whatever he does, he's got to walk from La Ferté, say another hour.'

'Fine!' said Picot. 'Now that we have some notion of the time, we can start asking questions. Did a man travelling alone arrive at La Ferté around two by bus or train? Did anyone on the road from La Ferté see a solitary man walking towards the car park in the clearing? We'll get a team of men on to it first thing tomorrow.'

'Who will remember?' said Raynal gloomily. 'It's days ago now.'

'Nobody, Michel. But a lot of fuss and activity at this end will keep Vautrin happy while we see what we can find out at Fleury.'

'Fleury is forbidden territory!' Raynal protested, horrified.

'Don't torment yourself, Michel. Vautrin gave me per-

113

mission to go there. He had to. The fibres from the car must be checked against Greenwood's clothes.'

Next morning they set out early for Fleury, taking Helène Rougemont from Forensics with them. She was to examine the contents of the wardrobe and see if a match could be found.

Just outside the village Picot stopped at what was evidently the local garage and filling station, and asked who if anyone in the neighbourhood owned an off-white Renault 5. After enumerating several which were the wrong colour, the proprietor named only two. One, a two-door, belonged to the priest, who was in his sixties, and the other, a four-door, to Madame de Fleury at the château.

'She drives it herself?'

The *garagiste* recoiled in mock alarm. '*Non, Dieu merçi!* She is a very old lady. There is a gardener who drives her, Philippe Dupont.'

Picot drove on, trying to suppress his excitement. For some hours a fantastic little suspicion had been bobbing about in his mind. One must not jump to conclusions, he told himself. The Renault 5 was a very popular model, millions of them had been produced. But he was entitled to take note of any fact which might be relevant: there was a Renault 5 at the Château de Fleury and a gardener who drove it.

Something in his expression alarmed Raynal. 'Jacques, take care,' he said in a near-whisper, so that Helène from Forensics in the back of the car would not overhear. 'Do not let yourself be mesmerized by a coincidence. It was dangerous even to ask.'

'I had my reasons.'

'Reasons which Vautrin's thought police forbid you to entertain.'

'Perhaps, but compelling ones.'

'*Nom de Dieu*, Jacques, what reasons are so compelling that we must risk our careers?'

'At a more opportune moment I will tell you,' Picot murmured. Helène might not be one of Vautrin's spies, but one never knew.

114

With Raynal grumbling ominously, they drove on into the village and up the avenue to the château. Antoinette, the housekeeper, opened the door for them, and Madame de Fleury met them in the hall. Asked how their enquiries were progressing, Picot said that they had made little progress. The theft of Miss Greenwood's letters was an unfortunate handicap.

'But I read the letters myself, Monsieur. I assure you that there was nothing in them which would have been of the slightest assistance to you. They were concerned mainly with the details of her botanical work.'

So unless she and Madame Grant were both lying, Picot thought, there was nothing in the letters worth withholding from the eyes of the judicial police.

'Our only conclusion so far,' he said, 'is that an off-white Renault Five was seen near the scene of the crime at the time of the murder.'

'How curious, Monsieur. It happens that my car is a Renault Five, and it is whitish in colour.'

Picot threw up his hands to suggest amazement. 'What a coincidence! Although the question is a laughable one, may I ask you as a matter of form where the car was on the Sunday of Miss Greenwood's death?'

'I was away from home, so I can't tell you. But I imagine it was in its usual parking place here.'

'No one drives it apart from yourself?'

'Oh, I never learnt how to drive. When I want to go somewhere, Philippe Dupont, my housekeeper's son, drives me.'

'He has the use of the car while you are away, Madame?'

She paused. 'If he wanted it for any reason, I would give permission. But he had his own means of transport, a powerful motorcycle.'

The mention of the motorcycle provoked a train of thought which would have to be followed later. He had noticed on the way in that the Renault was not among the cars in the parking bay, and asked where it was.

'It is not there, Monsieur, because my granddaughter

115

decided to go away on a visit, and asked Philippe to drive her.'

Picot led the party upstairs to Miss Greenwood's bedroom. As Hélène started work on the contents of the wardrobe, Picot stood listening at the door. When he heard Madame de Fleury leave the hall below, he began to tiptoe towards the stairs.

'Jacques, where are you going?' Raynal asked sharply.

'To ask Antoinette Dupont whether her son Philippe has an alibi for that Sunday.'

'You're mad. What will Vautrin say if he finds out what you're up to?'

'With luck, he won't.'

He found Antoinette peeling vegetables in a cool stone-flagged kitchen, and put the question. 'Your son is not here, Madame. Purely as a matter of routine, we would like to know how he spent his day on the Sunday before last.'

Antoinette wiped her hands nervously on her apron. 'But that was the day the English lady was murdered.'

'I repeat, Madame, that this is purely a matter of routine. We want to eliminate as many people as possible from our enquiries.'

It took her a little time to remember. 'Let me see. He got up late, on Sundays he likes a lazy morning. Then he did his exercises as usual, he never omits them. They take over an hour. After lunch he went out, I don't know where.'

An alibi for the morning was enough to clear him, but how sound was it? 'Did anyone besides yourself see him before he went out?'

'No,' she said after a moment's thought. 'A woman came from the village with eggs, but that was before he was up.'

'No one else?'

'Someone may have come while I was away at mass,' she murmured, 'but you'll have to ask Philippe.'

116

'If necessary we will do so when he returns. Do you know when that will be?'

'No, Monsieur.' She hesitated. 'I do not expect him to come back for a time. Philippe and Mademoiselle Anne-Marie have gone away together.'

'Gone away? You mean, they're runaway lovers?'

She was shocked. 'No, Monsieur, he is a good boy, he knows his place, he would never dream of attempting anything improper. Mademoiselle Anne-Marie had a quarrel with her family, and asked him to accompany her when she decided to leave the house.'

Wondering whether to believe this, Picot pressed on with the matter in hand. 'Did he have permission to use Madame de Fleury's car? Did he go anywhere in it on that Sunday, when she was away?'

She was staring at him in horror. Evidently she had been listening to the radio, which was still broadcasting appeals for the owner of a whitish four-door Renault 5 to come forward.

'He is innocent, Monsieur,' she wailed. 'He is a good boy, it is madness to suspect him.'

'I have no special reason to suspect him, Madame. I repeat, these are routine enquiries, we are putting the same questions to hundreds of people. Did your son take the Renault when he went out on that Sunday?'

'No!' she cried. 'He would never have used it without Madame's permission.'

'So when he went out in the afternoon, he was on foot?'

'No, on his motorcycle. You must believe me, Monsieur, he is innocent. Truly.'

She was wildly agitated now, and Picot himself began to be alarmed. He was not supposed to be interviewing the Fleury household at all, and Vautrin would be furious if he knew that he was driving the woman into a panic. He began making ineffective attempts to calm her down.

Upstairs, Helène had finished examining the contents of the wardrobe, and comparing them with the strands of green polyester and wool recovered from the car. Accompanied by Raynal, she joined him downstairs to make her report.

'There's nothing in the wardrobe that corresponds, Inspector. Nothing at all.'

'And in the *commode*?' Picot asked.

But the chest of drawers too had yielded nothing.

'So the fibres must have come from a garment of the murderer's,' Picot insisted.

'From a garment of some other person who drove the car,' she corrected pedantically.

Picot took Raynal aside. 'Madame Dupont can't give her son an alibi for the afternoon. She says he was here all morning, but there's no confirmation. Let's have a look at his clothes while we've got Forensics here. Call her and make her show us his room.'

Raynal went, and returned with Antoinette. 'She's hysterical already,' he murmured gloomily. 'She'll fly off her hinges if you suggest it.'

'Let her. He hasn't got an alibi, and he had access to an off-white Renault Five.'

'OK, if you say so, Jacques, but Vautrin's hinges will fly in our faces if he finds out.'

Told what was to happen, Antoinette burst into loud and tearful protest, but was made to lead the way across the courtyard to the Dupont quarters above the stables.

Philippe Dupont's bedroom was not large. In addition to his bed and storage for his clothes it contained an exercise bicycle, a rowing machine, various smaller muscle-enhancing devices, and on the wall, a very large photograph of Philippe wearing nothing but a *cache-sexe* and displaying what had resulted from the use of these appliances.

'Your son, Madame?'

'Yes, Monsieur,' admitted Antoinette tearfully. 'Though he is so strong, he is as gentle as a lamb.'

Because of serious overcrowding in the limited space, Helène made the two detectives wait outside while she

118

worked systematically through Philippe's clothes. Outside, Raynal attacked Picot at once. 'Jacques, you are mad. This will have us dismissed from the force.'

'I have my reasons, let me explain. Do you remember a case ten years ago or more, which the press called "The Affair of the Monster with the Van"?'

'Vaguely. I was still at school. Why?'

'So was I, but I read about it. The son of some château people were involved, and I'm pretty sure the château in question was Fleury.'

'How, "involved"?'

Picot began telling him, but he was too panic stricken to listen. 'You're running all these risks because you think it happened at Fleury, but you're not sure?'

'Pretty sure. To calm your fears, I shall get the dossier out of archives this afternoon, and check.'

'But even if you're right, what possible connection can there be between that nasty business and Greenwood being killed in a wood miles from here?'

'I don't know, but if there is a connection it is our duty to find it.'

The Forensics lady had finished her examination of Philippe's clothes. His chest of drawers had yielded a pullover which was roughly the right colour, but when it was impounded for more detailed examination in the laboratory, Antoinette burst into yet more protests that her son was innocent. Her loud lamentations were still going on when the party emerged into the courtyard. Raynal was horrified. At any moment the mistress of the house would come out and demand to know what was going on. There would be a row, which would reach the ears of Vautrin.

The central door of the château opened. But the person who came out was Celia Grant, with a letter she intended to post in the village. Antoinette ran across the courtyard towards her, shouting something.

'Goodness, what's wrong?' Celia asked, seeing her tear-stained face.

119

Antoinette explained that her Philippe was being accused of murdering Miss Greenwood. 'And now they have taken away his pullover to look for bloodstains.'

'No, really, Antoinette, how ridiculous. Let me speak to them.'

She went over to Picot and took him aside. 'You aren't considering Philippe Dupont seriously as a suspect?'

'There is circumstantial evidence, and he seems to have no alibi.'

'But he can't have killed Jane Greenwood. He's incapable of rape.'

'Many men are thought to be incapable of rape till it happens.'

'According to the family here he's not interested in women, nor even in men, they say he's unable to perform the sexual act. He's one of those men who devote themselves frenetically to physical culture, to develop their muscles, and spend their leisure admiring their own physique. Sex doesn't interest him. He's believed to use those chemicals . . . goodness, what d'you call them in French?'

'*Stéroïdes*, Madame?'

'That's right, and you know what they do to men.'

Picot was intrigued. 'This is strange knowledge for a lady visitor from England to possess. How, please, did you acquire it?'

'I'm only repeating what two members of the family have told me. Do stop this ridiculous business and tell poor Antoinette to stop tormenting herself.'

But Picot was not prepared to be ordered about by a foreign woman barely five feet tall. 'I have already explained to her that innocent people have nothing to fear from our enquiries,' he said, and started walking towards his car.

But she was not ready to let him go. Her position at the château was becoming more awkward every minute. She had decided to cut and run. As soon as she could get Jane safely buried, she would head for home.

'One moment, Inspector,' she called. 'Can you tell me

when Miss Greenwood's body will be released for burial?'

He turned back. 'On my return to headquarters I will speak to the pathologist concerned.'

'Please do, and could you ask him to hurry up? I'm only here still because no one else seems to be responsible for the arrangements, and I'm anxious to get home.'

They stood there, facing each other. For a moment it seemed to Picot that she was going to say something more. If so, she had changed her mind, for she moved away with a curt nod, and went over to Antoinette to try to reassure her.

Once more, Picot had an impression that she was holding something back.

'A strange woman, Michel,' he said as he and Raynal drove away. 'She knows more than she tells us, of that I am sure.'

'What can she know?'

'I have no idea, but for the present I shall not let her bury Greenwood and go home. Greenwood can stay in the mortuary at the hospital till I know more.'

'On what pretext?'

'Let's say, I am not convinced that the injuries to the vagina have been sufficiently examined, and are probably inconsistent with rape.'

'If Madame Grant's information is correct,' Raynal reasoned, 'Dupont can't have raped Greenwood, because his family jewels don't function.'

'But he could still have killed her.'

'How so, Jacques?'

'You saw the photo, he is blond, he is appetizing to look at. That repressed English virgin is tempted, she loses her head and makes an imprudent approach. He is disgusted, he is *narcissiste*, whatever sexual instincts he has are perverted. He does not rape her, but in his repugnance he kills her and, as the autopsy suggests, he performs a ritual mutilation.'

121

'Having followed her to the Sologne for the purpose?' Raynal objected. 'You must be joking.'

'Perhaps I am. I shall drop you off at La Ferté to orchestrate activity at the incident centre which will keep Vautrin happy. Then I shall take Helène back to Orleans and get the file on the Monster with the Van out of Archives.'

Celia said what she could to calm Antoinette's fears, then went on to the village to post her letter. Her thoughts were gloomy. She had an appointment that afternoon with a Reformed Church pastor in Orleans to make provisional funeral arrangements, but when would Jane's remains be released for burial? The Inspector had been very vague when she asked. And incidentally, who was to foot the bill? Her replacement Visa card had just arrived by post, but she saw no reason to burden her account with huge payments to an undertaker. It was time Uncle Hugo's lawyers came up with some answers. She posted her letter, then went back to the château to telephone them.

The partner who was dealing with the problem proved to be a model of crisp efficiency. Miss Greenwood's will, he said, left everything absolutely to her mother. Her estate was less than fifty thousand pounds, excluding the value of the cottage, but there was a substantial insurance policy payable on death. She had appointed her mother as sole executor.

'If you like, Mrs Grant, I could arrange to remit a sum to France for the immediate funeral expenses, which of course are the first call on the estate. How much would you like?'

'Say a thousand?' said Celia, guessing wildly.

'By British standards that would be very little. I think I should make it two. I'll get a banker's draft sent off to you today.'

'Thank you. I suppose I have authority to bury her here?'

'Mrs Appleton, the sister-in-law from Leicestershire, raised no objection before she left to go home. Her only concern, I think, was to avoid being put to trouble or expense. Mrs Greenwood is in no position to express a view.'

'D'you know how she is?'

'I believe she has recovered her speech a little, and keeps asking for her daughter. They haven't had the heart to tell her the sad news.'

'Horrors. How awful.'

'A very sad situation, Mrs Grant, I agree.'

Celia could not help reflecting that her own situation, though far less sad than old Mrs Greenwood's, was far from cheerful. She was torn between conflicting impulses. Marooned far from home by her responsibility for the corpse of a comparative stranger, and filled with suspicions of a kind which no well-mannered guest should entertain, she was tempted at times to abandon Jane's corpse to its own devices and make a dash for home. On the other hand, mysteries fascinated her and this one was irresistible. There were moments when Jane's remains seemed to her a positive godsend, since they provided her with a cast-iron excuse for staying where she was till the case was solved.

Adrienne was busy writing letters in the salon. Unwilling to interrupt, Celia went up to the library for another look at Paul-Henri's drawings. There were several hundred, each illustrating half a dozen plants of the same family. They were magnificent, but they covered less than half the species and sub-species of the French flora, which accounted for over five thousand entries in Bonnier. True to the brief she had been given, Jane had gone to work with her portable typewriter and produced sheet after sheet of meticulous descriptions of each plant in the technical language of botany. She had also noted down the flowering time and the type of habitat in which it was likely to be found, and Celia wondered at first how an English botanist unfamiliar with France had managed this.

Then she remembered. All she had to do was to refer to Paul-Henri's herbarium specimens, each labelled with the date and place of collection, consult the corresponding entry in the *Flora Europaea* and write up the result.

Jane's mass of notes was of course in English. It would have to be translated, and Celia wondered yet again why Adrienne had not made a more determined effort to recruit a French botanist to do the job.

Angry voices were coming from somewhere outside. She went to the open window of the library, which gave a bird's-eye view over the entrance court. Adrienne's Renault was back. And standing on the entrance steps below was Philippe Dupont, in furious argument with Adrienne who was out of sight in the doorway but unmistakable in voice. It was impossible to hear everything they were saying, but snatches that floated up suggested that she was fighting to get her precious Anne-Marie out of his clutches. She was getting nowhere. Philippe was losing his temper and had begun to shout. 'You will regret this. I shall make you crawl, I shall make you swallow grass snakes because of the way you have treated me.'

Leaving the Renault standing in the middle of the courtyard, he strode into the stable block. When he came out, he was wheeling a large powerful-looking motorcycle, which could easily have been the one that the bag-snatchers in Orleans had used. He kick-started it with furious movements. It sprang into life, and he roared away.

When Celia came downstairs at lunch time she found Adrienne sitting in the salon, obviously very upset, for her hands were twitching in her lap and she was staring into vacancy. 'Philippe has been here.'

'Yes, so I saw.'

'He came to bring the car back. But he won't tell me where he has taken poor Anne-Marie.'

'He won't harm her, will he?' said Celia.

'I think he will try to use her in some underhand way to force us to recognize him as Jean-Louis' son. He almost said as much.'

When they sat down to lunch, she picked silently at her food and ate hardly anything. Antoinette handed round the dishes with a set face and puffy eyes, and had obviously been crying.

Halfway through the meal Hortense burst into the room. 'Adrienne!' she shouted. 'What's this I hear? You let him escape, that *voyou*, that *crapule*?'

'What did you expect me to do? We have no dungeon here at Fleury.'

'Why did you not keep him here and send for the police and make him tell them where he has hidden my poor little Anne-Marie?'

'Hortense, you are a fool. Anne-Marie is eighteen years old. She went away with him of her own accord. When she is sick of him, which will be very soon, she will come back.'

'But by then what fate will she have suffered!'

'With Philippe? You know as well as I do that that's nonsense.'

'Adrienne, you have no heart. You have no conception of what a mother feels when her daughter is in danger.'

'Oh really, must we have melodrama? What "danger" are you afraid of?'

'He will poison her mind against me.'

'Nonsense, you'd poisoned it yourself long ago, by screaming at her and bullying her, there's no more poisoning left for Philippe to do.'

'Be careful how you insult me! A little politeness please, or you will regret it.'

Adrienne rang a little handbell for Antoinette. 'Enough of this, our *soufflé au Cointreau* will be going flat. Sit down and have some, or leave us in peace to enjoy it.'

'I mean what I say, Adrienne,' Hortense screamed. 'It is I who pay for everything. When the roof of the château is leaking you come to me. When Emile cannot pay his share of the upkeep, it is I who foot the bill. Whenever money is needed, you all come to me, without me, you could not continue to live here. I throw money out of the window to keep you all in comfort, yet you

125

insult me and despise me for my pains, so why should I continue?'

'Because you are an idiotic goose of a bourgeoise, who thinks it is heaven to be called de Fleury de Marcilly, and would pay anything for the privilege. Don't wave your moneybags at me, but go, before I throw something at you. You shall have no *soufflé au Cointreau*, you do not deserve it.'

'It would make me vomit,' shouted Hortense, and swept out, slamming the door.

Adrienne grimaced. 'It is bad enough without recitatives and arias from her.'

The *soufflé* arrived, but in the tense atmosphere it did not have the success it probably deserved. After Adrienne's spirited rebuke to Hortense she had relapsed into gloom. Celia helped herself sparingly and toyed with her plateful, for it would have been heartless to eat with relish in the presence of Adrienne's obvious distress: she had taken half a spoonful, and pushed it around her plate for a time. Then, telling Antoinette to serve coffee on the terrace, she rose. 'Celia, my dear, I am not in the mood for coffee. If you will excuse me I will go upstairs at once for my siesta.'

Celia settled down on the terrace. A grim-faced Antoinette brought out her coffee on to the terrace and deposited the tray. 'Madame . . .'

'Yes, Antoinette?'

'There is something I wish to ask you. Tell me, please, the name of the policeman who comes here and asks questions.'

'That was Inspector Picot. He comes from Orleans.'

'From the Commissariat there?'

'That's right, Antoinette. Why d'you want to know?'

'There is something that I think the police should be told. According to the news on the radio, the car of the man who killed Mademoiselle Greenwood was a pale-coloured Renault Five, like Madame's car.'

Celia knew this, having read it in a brief news item

in *Le Figaro*. She wondered what was coming next.

'The police asked me whether my Philippe went out in Madame's car on that Sunday,' Antoinette went on. 'He did not, but someone else did. Monsieur Emile drove away in it soon after Mademoiselle Greenwood left, poor lady, to go to the place where she was killed.' She paused significantly. 'And he did not return till the evening.'

I am not hearing this, Celia told herself, it is not happening. I am becoming everybody's confidante, and have no means of knowing which of them, if any, is telling the truth.

She was sick of all this carry-on. There was no making sense of any of it, the inner workings of the Fleury household were quite beyond her. Suddenly she longed to be back at Archerscroft, hybridizing hellebores.

SEVEN

Having finished her coffee, Celia felt an urgent need for a change of air, and spent a pleasant half-hour exploring the woodland which lay beyond the enclosing hornbeam hedge of the formal garden. When she turned back to the château, Antoinette was standing on the terrace, obviously on the look-out for her.

When Celia joined her there, she drew her into the house and spoke in a low voice. 'While you were out, Madame, Mademoiselle Anne-Marie telephoned and asked to speak to you.'

'Oh, how is she?'

'Well, I think.' Antoinette gave her a conspiratorial look. 'She begs you to visit her, but without letting Madame know, or any of the others.'

'Where is Madame?'

'Still asleep.'

'And where is Mademoiselle Anne-Marie?'

'At the Château de Premay with her friend Mademoiselle de Saint-Amand.'

'And is Philippe there with her?'

'No, Madame.'

'Did she mention a time?'

'No, Madame. Whenever you can come. She will wait for you.'

'Then I shall go now. When Madame finishes her siesta and comes down, you could tell her that I have had a message from Orleans from the firm of *pompes funèbres* dealing with the arrangements about Miss Greenwood, and have gone to see about it.'

Antoinette permitted herself a thin, rather malicious smile. 'Very good, Madame. But before you go, Monsieur André is in the kitchen. He would like to speak to you.'

'Oh. Very well,' said Celia, wondering how many more members of the family were going to confide in her. She found him sitting at the kitchen table, looking young, healthy, uncomplicated, and incapable of deceit. Having encountered several appallingly wicked young men of equally innocent appearance, she was not disarmed and asked him what he wanted.

'Antoinette has told me, Madame, that you know where Anne-Marie is and are going to see her.'

'Yes,' Celia replied, wondering if there was any limit to Antoinette's capacity for intrigue.

'I would be grateful if you would take her a message.'

'Of course.'

But instead of producing a letter as she expected, he hesitated. 'It is not really a message. It is more . . . well, if you could explain something to her. The reason why I had a secret that I couldn't share with her.'

Silence.

'Well? I am listening.'

'I am very fond of her, you see. When she became angry because I wouldn't confide in her I was in despair, I was confused, I could not explain myself properly.'

She saw now that he was genuinely distressed. 'André, what do you want me to say to Anne-Marie?'

'I don't know really . . . You could explain that it isn't my secret, and I'm not allowed to tell anyone, but it will make a huge difference to me. If everything goes right, it means that in the autumn I shall be able to go to Paris and study law, instead of struggling with that ridiculous farm.'

'But, André, what do I say when she asks me why this happy turn of events has to be treated as a profound secret?'

He looked miserable. 'There's nothing you can say. That's the difficulty.'

'It seems to me,' Celia decided, 'that the best thing I can do is to tell her that you're fond of her and very upset, and hope you can be friends again soon.'

'If you tell her that it will be marvellous,' said André with a relieved grin. 'Thank you.'

As she drove away to meet Anne-Marie she thought about this conversation, and tried to build on it a scenario about what might have happened. It looked as if Emile had laid hands on a substantial sum of money by rather dishonest means. André seemed to know about this, and his silence had apparently been bought with a suggestion that his parents' new-found affluence would make it possible for him to stop farming and study law. But there was no question of letting anyone else in on the secret, certainly not a girl with an upright conscience like Anne-Marie.

How could André have found out about the illegal windfall? And even more puzzling, how could the news of it have reached Jean-Louis? Presumably that was what he and Emile had been quarrelling about while Adrienne was away with Hortense at the spa.

But they had stopped quarrelling and formed a secret alliance; why? In order to go bag-snatching together on Philippe's motorcycle and recover Jane's letters? But even if they had murdered Jane, there was no reason why they should regard the letters as a threat. They had both read them and knew that they contained nothing incriminating. The whole thing did not make sense.

But Antoinette said she had seen Emile drive away in pursuit of Jane on the fatal Sunday. If she was telling the truth, he was the murderer. If Jean-Louis fitted in at all, he was an accomplice. But an unanswerable question followed. Why had Emile wanted to kill Jane?

With the help of the map and Antoinette's directions, she arrived at the Château de Premay just after three. It was smaller than Fleury and in rather bad repair. Sounds of people playing tennis came from somewhere in the grounds. But before she could start to explore, Anne-

130

Marie came out of the front door to meet her.

'Oh, *génial*, Celia! Thank you for coming.' She led the way to a seat overlooking a straggly box parterre. 'We can talk, the others are all out riding or playing tennis. *Grand-mère* doesn't know you're here?'

'No, but André does, Antoinette told him I was coming. He gave me a message for you.'

Undeterred by Anne-Marie's sulky frown, Celia discharged her mission on André's behalf as best she could, but Anne-Marie was not appeased. 'I know what's happened, it's clear as mud. Uncle Emile's desperate for money, his factory's on the verge of bankruptcy. And now he's found some dirty way of making a bit of cash, where money's concerned he's as slippery as an eel. For some reason he needs André to give him a hand, so he's told André that if he shuts his eyes to whatever louche business they're involved in, he can study law and forget that silly farm.'

'How d'you know that Emile's firm is heading for bankruptcy?'

'André says so. He says *Maman* has come to the rescue twice already, and of course she makes herself very unpleasant when she has to hand out the money. That's why André has to farm, Aunt Chantal thinks that every penny she can scrape together makes her less dependent on *Maman*.'

'Your mother's a rich woman, is she?'

'Yes, *richissime*, her father made a fortune from washing-machines.'

'But I don't understand why your uncle and aunt quarrelled with your parents,' Celia objected.

'That's easy. Papa's found out what Uncle Emile's doing. He's suffered a lot from Uncle Emile's slimy way with money, and this time he's decided it's absolutely too smelly and indelicate to be swallowed.'

But that explanation, Celia reflected, did not explain why Emile and Jean-Louis had secretly become reconciled, while still pretending to be enemies.

131

'I suppose *Maman*'s white with fury at me,' said Anne-Marie. 'Don't tell her where I am or she'll drag me back on the end of a chain to go to that wretched *rallye*. I wanted to ask you, can I really come to England and work in your nursery?'

'Of course, if your parents agree. I'll try to fix it with them when things are a bit calmer.'

'*Ouais super!* They'll agree. Anything to get me out of the way. And I must escape, I can't stay at Fleury with André sulking and Philippe a broken reed.'

'Philippe isn't at Fleury. He came, but he left again at once in a huff, after your grandmother gave him a talking to.'

'She's probably as fed up with him as I am.' Anne-Marie grimaced. 'I dumped him, because he turns out to be mad. Absolutely *cinglé*.'

'Horrors. What happened?'

'Well, I'd only decamped with him because I was blind with anger against mother and the whole bazaar at Fleury, I hadn't thought about what was to happen next. He was supposed to find out for me what André's great secret was about, and why it had set off such a stinking family quarrel, and I didn't see how he was going to do it. So after a bit I asked him to stop somewhere so we could make some plans. He drew up at a little café, and we settled down to talk over an espresso. But instead of planning anything he started on a long blablabla about how unkind the family was to him and how unfair it was of them not to recognize him as a Fleury and treat him as an equal. I didn't interrupt because I agree, it is unfair and I know he feels strongly about it, so I thought I'd better let him get it off his chest.'

'Fair enough.'

'Yes, but wait. After a bit he got up and said, "Come." I said, "Where to?" But instead of telling me he got me into the car and drove off. We ended up in a rather low quarter of Orleans, and he took me into a louche sort of bistro full of very odd-looking men with very chic

132

coiffures and lots of bulging muscles in rather revealing singlets. They were obviously buddies of Philippe's, because when he came in he said, "*Salut les mecs,*" and they all shook hands with him and said, "*Hé mec.*"

'After a bit it dawned on me that I was being shown off as his girlfriend. He kept putting his arm round me and making rather suggestive jokes and at one stage he even threatened to take off his shirt so that I could feel his biceps. I wasn't having that, and I'd begun to feel uncomfortable because this roomful of very peculiar men seemed to be having some secret joke at my expense. So I said I was hungry, so could we go somewhere and eat? But he said we could eat there and ordered us hamburgers which was all they seemed to have, and when we sat down to eat them he started again on his blablabla against the family.

'After that there were a lot more suggestive jokes, and some of them were quite disgusting. What was worse, four of the *mecs* were sitting at the table with us and laughing behind their hands. So I got up and said I wasn't going to accept any more of that, and would Philippe please get me a taxi. But he went on eating and took no notice, and I wasn't going to go out looking for one in that area of Orleans, no thank you. So in the end I abandoned myself to the mercy of the barman, who had earrings and his shirt open down to the navel but was quite nice really, and he got me a cab. I took it to the station and got a train to Beaugency, and the Saint-Amands collected me from there.'

'What an alarming experience,' said Celia.

'Yes. I knew Philippe was weird, but not as weird as that.'

'I'm sorry it turned out so badly. What d'you propose to do now?'

Anne-Marie's plans turned out to be cut and dried. She would stay where she was for long enough to escape having to attend the *rallye*. As soon as possible after that she would take up Celia's offer of a summer job at

133

Archerscroft nurseries. 'I can come?' she repeated. 'You really mean it?'

Celia assured her that of course she meant it, and took her leave. Heading back to Fleury, she wondered how good Anne-Marie would be at pricking out hellebore seedlings. But it was not in her nature to be unkind to the deserving young.

Back at Fleury she found Adrienne waiting for her eagerly. 'Ah, my dear, I am glad that your business in Orleans did not take too long. I have an errand to perform, and that wicked Philippe is not here to drive me.'

'I'll take you, of course.'

'Oh, thank you. Today is the anniversary of my poor Edouard's death, and I must put these on his tomb.'

She picked up an elaborate floral confection, clearly ordered from an expensive shop, which stood on a side table. Celia declined the offer of the unfamiliar Renault with its left-hand drive, and they set out in her own car to the cemetery, which lay some distance outside the village.

Halfway there, as they rounded a bend with a steep bank on one side of the road, Adrienne suddenly plunged her face in her hands. 'Oh! I can never bear to pass that place. When I'm in my own car I'm on the right-hand side beside Philippe, and I turn my head so I don't see it.'

'Something happened there?' Celia asked.

'It is there that my poor Paul-Henri ran off the road and was killed.'

'How awful. What happened exactly?'

'It was late at night. He was alone, and he lost control, we think there was something wrong with the steering. It was a terrible old van, like a heap of metal from the scrap yard. Edouard offered several times to replace it, but Paul-Henri refused. He was fond of that rattly old *casserole*, but in the end it killed him.'

She was looking pale and shaken. Even after all these years, she had to turn away when she passed the place where her beloved botanist son had died.

The cemetery, surrounded by a high wall, lay among

open fields. Celia parked by the roadside. Adrienne got out of the car and walked in through the wrought-iron gates, carrying the flowers. Celia began to follow.

Adrienne turned. 'My dear, there is no need for you to come.'

As Celia hesitated, Adrienne's blue eyes were suddenly full of tears. 'No, please, Celia. I would rather be alone.'

After a few minutes she came back. 'We must hurry home now, to be in time for the *curé*'s visit. He always comes on the anniversary, in theory to express his condolences, but in reality because I always give him a donation and a glass of port.'

The *curé* duly appeared at the front door, and Celia made to withdraw so that spiritual comfort could be administered. But that seemed not to be on the agenda.

'In the name of Heaven, don't go, my dear!' Adrienne murmured. 'Stay and give me support. He's a frightful old bore and he always stays for the ritual half-hour, and I can never think of enough things to say to him. *Ah, mon père, que vous êtes gentil de venir me voir.*'

He sat down and Antoinette brought port. Adrienne's prediction of a sticky half-hour was not fulfilled, because Jane Greenwood's untimely demise and Celia's connection with her provided a ready made and all-absorbing subject of conversation.

After a time the *curé* turned to practical matters. 'Perhaps, Madame, I may profit from my visit to discuss the unfortunate lady's funeral arrangements.'

'Miss Greenwood was not a Catholic,' said Adrienne quickly.

The *curé* turned enquiringly to Celia, who said that Jane was an Anglican, but could not make the claim with much conviction. 'I am in touch with the pastor of the Reformed Church in Orleans, who knows of a graveyard there which will agree to receive her.'

The *curé* was shocked. 'Why not here, near to the house where she passed her last days, near to her friends here? The time is long past when a village cemetery like ours

135

was closed to Christians of another confession.'

'Arrangements have already been made elsewhere,' said Adrienne quickly.

'Actually, no,' Celia corrected. 'Nothing's been fixed yet, and I'd much rather she was buried here.'

The *curé* assured her that it would be perfectly in order for a pastor of the Reformed Church to perform the ceremony, and asked when what he called the "*dépouille mortelle*' would be released for burial by the authorities.

'Any moment now,' said Celia, 'so perhaps you could tell the gravedigger to get to work.'

'No doubt you would like to visit our peaceful little graveyard and choose your unfortunate friend's last resting place.'

'I shouldn't bother,' said Adrienne briskly. 'She can be put next to whoever was buried last.'

Slightly surprised, Celia agreed to this and the *curé* rose to go, after pocketing Adrienne's donation and saying that he would leave a note of the church dues for funerals on the hall table for Celia's attention.

Changing in her room before dinner, Celia focused her thoughts on the fact that Adrienne seemed to have some psychological hang-up about the village graveyard. Right at the beginning she had made what proved to be an unfounded suggestion that the church authorities would not let Jane be accommodated there. Just now, when depositing the flowers on her husband's grave, she had prevented Celia from following her. Her interventions during the *curé*'s visit had been directed to the same end: to keep Celia out of the graveyard if possible. What was there in it that she did not want Celia to see?

Left in charge of the incident centre at La Ferté, Raynal was working his way through a pile of statements from the public which led nowhere when a policewoman ushered in a very unsavoury informant with a three-day growth of beard, dirty working clothes, and a strong smell of sour red wine. He had arrived in one of the noisy little three-wheeled load-carrying vehicles which French peasants use as beasts of burden on the farm as well as for road travel, and in view of his far from sober condition, it was a miracle that he had arrived at La Ferté safely.

On entering the room, he ogled the departing police-woman lustfully. 'I bet she has a nice little apricot, that one.'

'Shut your gob!' snapped Raynal, scandalized. 'I'm not listening to that sort of dirty talk. Who are you, and what d'you want?'

His name, he said, was Jean Sorel and he lived on a smallholding just outside Fleury. It soon became clear that he had come only to air an irrelevant grievance: a farm called La Roulandière, which should rightly have been his, had been stolen from him by 'that female vampire Marchant at the château'. He went on confusedly for some time about the bloodsucking tendencies of the Fleury family, till Raynal became impatient. 'What's this got to do with the Englishwoman's murder?'

'A lot, you wait.'

Raynal waited, but Sorel rambled off into yet another diatribe against Chantal Marchant, mixed up with an obscure grievance about a well.

Raynal cut him short. 'What about this well?' he asked. 'Where is it?'

'Where d'you think? On La Roulandière, that those *saligauds* stole from me. Right by the cottage, it was.'

'What do you say they did to this well?'

'That imbecile of a boy wrecked it.'

'Be more precise. Who do you say wrecked it?'

'The son of the Marchant witch. An ignorant little mother's boy who knows nothing of farming. When she stole the farm from me she gave it to him to muck about with, and that's what he's done, good and proper. Disorder and shitty incompetence everywhere! Good clean land let go sour! Don't even know there's an old well in the yard, so he drives his tractor over it and *hop*! The

137

planks over the well-head give and he's got his front wheels halfway down the well.'

'But what has this to do with the matter I am investigating?'

'All in good time, don't be in such a hurry and I'll tell you. There was things down that well, things that ought to be mine by rights, and those bastards at the château found them and stole them.'

'What sort of things?'

'Money. Papers showing that my cousin intended me to have the farm.'

'Did you see them taking these things out of the well?'

'No. They're too cunning.'

'Then how d'you know?'

'Marcel saw them. He saw them do it, and he told me.'

By slow degrees Raynal extracted the story from him. With the tractor poised precariously over the well, André Marchant had gone in a panic to get help from his uncle. Jean-Louis de Fleury had come to the rescue in his van, bringing with him a chain and tackle, and Marcel Naudet, one of his labourers, to help. After they had tried for a time to pull the tractor out, it was time for Marcel's lunch break and de Fleury had sent him home to eat.

'That was their cunning, you see,' Sorel explained. 'They didn't want no witnesses to see what they was up to.'

When Marcel got back, André and his uncle had managed to drag the tractor to safety. 'But Marcel, he has sharp eyes, he has. Saw through their little game. He spotted a box in the back of the van, quite a big tin box all dirty with earth, that hadn't been there before, and when that Jean-Louis sees Marcel coming, he pops his jacket over it quick to hide it. And Marcel, he had to walk back to the field he'd been called away from. He don't get a lift in the van, for fear he'll take another look at that box.'

Sorel leaned forward for emphasis, enveloping Raynal in a cloud of foul breath. 'Now, why am I telling you this story of the wrong they done to me, stealing that box?

Not because I hope to get my rights, no one can when there's château people on the take. But murder's different, you can't let them get away with that.'

'Murder?'

'The Englishwoman, the one you're on about, that's got herself measured for a wooden costume. That lot at the château, they killed her.'

'Why would they want to do that?'

He raised an unsteady finger in a sly gesture to the side of his nose. 'They had to kill her because she saw the box too, and knew they were stealing it. They were afraid she'd tell me.'

'How d'you know she was there? Did Naudet see her?'

Sorel looked sulky. 'Might have done.'

In other words he didn't, Raynal thought, this is guess-work based on malice.

'Anyway, I know they're the guilty ones,' Sorel added. 'I saw one of them drive off that Sunday morning in the old woman's Renault.'

'Oh. Which one?'

A moment's pause. 'It was Marchant. The little prick's father.'

'What time was this?' Raynal asked, startled.

'In the morning.'

'What time in the morning?'

A vague gesture. 'Early.'

He doesn't know the right time to say, Raynal thought, and he's got a grudge against the Marchants. And if his breath on a weekday is any guide, he would have been too pie-eyed and wooden-mouthed on a Sunday morning to see a car, let alone identify its driver. Dismissing him, Raynal said: 'Try to sober up a bit before you drive home.'

Picot's visit to the Archives at the Commissariat had left him angry and puzzled. The file about the so called Monster with the Van was not in the Archives. But he could not break the news to Raynal when he reached the incident centre at La Ferté, because more immediate

139

matters claimed his attention. A bicycle with an auxiliary motor was leaning up against the wall outside the gendarmerie. Inside stood its owner, a girl in her late teens.

'She's been waiting almost an hour,' Raynal murmured, 'so would you see her at once? Her mother doesn't know she's here, and she's afraid of being missed.'

'What's the story?'

'She won't say. She'll only tell you.'

Picot took her into the inner room and studied her. She was flat-chested and scrawny, with freckles and sandy hair. She said her name was Dominique Custine, and that she lived with her parents at a farm just outside Fleury.

'And you have come all this way to give me information?'

'I thought it my duty, Monsieur. But my situation is very embarrassing. You won't tell my mother?'

'No, Mademoiselle Dominique, you can rely on my discretion.'

'And I won't have to give evidence in court?'

'It depends on the nature of your information, but I doubt it.'

'Very well, Monsieur.' She took a deep breath, and cast her eyes down modestly. 'Philippe cannot have been guilty of this crime. He spent that afternoon with me.'

'How long was he with you, Dominique?'

'He came at three, and we were together till supper time.'

'At your house?'

'Oh no, Monsieur.' The downcast eyes came modestly into play again. 'We were in my uncle's barn.'

'Did anyone see you there?'

'Oh no! We were very careful not to be seen. My parents would have half killed me if they'd known.'

Picot felt very sorry for her. Even if Madame Grant was wrong and Philippe's masculine attributes were capable of doing their job, she would have needed to display an enormous aura of sexual prosperity to make her story credible. On the contrary, she had the doomed look of an unattractive girl who was destined to form an unrequited passion for any handsome man in sight. But it would be cruel to tell her to stop her nonsense and go away. She must be allowed her dream of imaginary rapture on a hot Sunday afternoon. He took a solemn note of her testimony and sent her home.

'What was all that about?' Raynal asked when she had mounted her bicycle and gone.

'She says Dupont was busy stuffing her in a barn that afternoon, so he can't have murdered Greenwood.'

They burst into loud laughter.

'Antoinette must have put her up to it,' said Picot. 'She knew the silly girl had a *béguin* for her Philippe, so she sent her all this way to prop up his alibi with her self-sacrifice.'

'I wish mother Dupont would calm down,' grumbled Raynal, 'or she'll have us in trouble with Vautrin.'

'We can't help it if people from Fleury come to us here and tell us fairy stories.'

'Jacques, you don't seriously think Dupont's guilty?'

'I can't see a motive. But I'm sure someone at Fleury's got one, more than ever now. D'you know what? I asked Archives for the file on the Monster with the Van, but it was out.'

'Out? Who was it marked out to?'

'Vautrin.'

They stared at each other in amazed conjecture.

'You see what this means,' said Picot. 'He's confiscated it. He knows there's a connection between Greenwood's death and that old horror story, and he took the file out in case we remembered about it and tried to follow it up.'

'Because of what the media would say if we did? I suppose he's terrified of a repeat of the Bettencourt scandal.'

'I think it's worse than that. He's a supporter of wealth and privilege, he's protecting the family at Fleury because he's afraid of what we'd unearth if we started investigating.'

141

'No, Jacques. Be reasonable. What possible connection could there be between our affair and the death all those years ago of that miserable young man?'

'I've no idea. But if there is one it's our duty to find it, Vautrin or no Vautrin. It's time for lunch, let's forget about him for the moment in case he spoils our digestion.'

'I agree. Unless we get out of here, something else will happen to confuse the trails.'

The next instalment of confusion was not long delayed. Soon after the two detectives returned from consuming an excellent *boeuf en daube*, Antoinette Dupont came through on the telephone, having been given the La Ferté number by the police switchboard in Orleans. Before coming to the point, Antoinette protested that she did not want to cause trouble for anyone, but felt it was her duty to report what she knew: Emile Marchant had driven off in his mother's car on the Sunday morning, and had not returned till evening.

'What time in the evening?' Picot asked.

She hesitated. 'Between six and seven.'

Picot was convinced that she had engineered the ridiculous confession by Dominique, and saw no reason to believe her accusation against Marchant. He thanked her solemnly for her information, and grinned despairingly at Raynal.

'What a *connerie* of a case, Michel. What have we got? A frightened woman who incriminates her employer to take the heat off her son; a silly girl who says she had an afternoon of rapture with a man whose marriage equipment is said to be no use at all; and a drunk with a grudge who invents a lunatic story.'

'How lunatic is it?' Picot wondered. 'There might be something real behind his fantasy about a well.'

'A well with a box in it?'

'It's possible, I suppose.'

'Containing something so valuable that they had to kill Greenwood because she found out? No, Jacques.'

'Nevertheless,' said Picot, 'I am sure the Château de Fleury is at the centre of the whole affair.'

Then what are we doing here in the Sologne?'

'Passing a comb through it for a non-existent sex-killer, to satisfy Vautrin.'

To placate the importunate judge, they started going through a mass of inconclusive scraps of information which had been phoned in to the incident centre. While they were so engaged Philippe Dupont arrived at the gendarmerie on his motorcycle and strode in, blond, handsome, and impressively muscular in a singlet and very tight jeans.

'My mother's a fool,' he told Picot, 'coming out with all that nonsense. I thought she knew where I was that afternoon.'

'Evidently she did not, Monsieur,' said Picot. 'So perhaps you will now inform us.'

He had been taking part, he explained, it what seemed from his description to have been a sort of beauty competition in Paris for muscle-men like himself. He gave the names and addresses of the organizer and several of the contestants, and although his alibi would have to be checked, it was obviously cast-iron.

'If we had had this information earlier,' Picot told him, 'we would have been saved trouble and your mother would have been spared much needless anxiety.'

'I told you, I thought she knew. Anyway, I had no idea I was under suspicion.'

'It is unfortunate that you were away from home.'

'In company with Madame de Fleury's granddaughter,' Raynal put in.

'Yes,' said Philippe, preening himself a little. 'You know, of course, that she is my sister. Is there anything more you want to ask me? No? Then good day, gentlemen.'

So saying, he stalked out of the room.

'*Ouf!*' said Raynal as the door closed behind him. 'Such arrogance, why does he say that Mademoiselle de Fleury is his sister?'

'He is a fantasist. He is also our only suspect, but has an alibi which will certainly prove irrefutable. As if all that false information from interested parties wasn't enough.'

'Was it all false, Jacques? Sorel and Madame Dupont both say they saw Emile Marchant driving away in the white Renault.'

'Sorel's a drunk with a grudge against the château. The Dupont woman would say anything to protect her son.'

'But she was right about the time the murderer would have got back after collecting his car.'

'Guesswork,' said Picot. 'Shall we ask her if she was lying? She might admit it, now that her darling's in the clear.'

'No, Jacques! D'you want her to complain to Vautrin that we bully her? Anyway, I'm sure she'd deny it.'

'She and Sorel both say the same thing,' Picot remarked. 'It's just possible it could be true.'

When they left the building, they had to run the gauntlet of journalists gathered outside, for the fact that Greenwood had been a guest at Fleury was now public knowledge. They shouted questions at Picot, and one of them, from a trouble-making Paris scandal-sheet, asked him mockingly if he intended to arrest any members of the Fleury family.

'There,' said Raynal anxiously as they drove off. 'You see what risks you are taking. They all remember the Bettencourt affair, and are determined to trap us again.'

'We are not here to conform to the prejudices of the media, but to bring guilty people to justice.'

'We've no evidence, Jacques, that anyone at Fleury's guilty.'

'Nevertheless we're going back to Fleury now, to ask a few questions in the village. I want to know if anyone else saw the Renault drive out of the gates there on that Sunday morning, and whether the motorcycle went out on the Thursday with a pillion passenger behind the rider. Who else besides Philippe Dupont owns a motorcycle? Do either Emile Marchant or Jean-Louis de Fleury know how to ride one? And where were those two on the days in question?'

'Who will tell us all this?'

'Gossips who frequent the bar in the Hôtel du Commerce. With luck they will also tell us what we failed to discover from the dossier which Vautrin has confiscated: what happened to the so-called Monster with the Van.'

Raynal quailed in alarm. 'Jacques, I hope you know what you're doing.'

'I do, Michel, I do.'

That night Celia lay awake for a long time, wondering whether or not she was letting her imagination run away with her. She already had one solid fact to go on, she had not imagined the secret collaboration between Emile and Jean-Louis. And now there was another certainty. Adrienne was trying to keep her out of the graveyard. There was something there that she did not want her to see.

What was it? Fortunately there was a simple way to find out. She would go and look.

Setting her alarm clock for six, she dressed and crept out of the house. It was a glorious morning. Rather than risk waking the household by starting her car she decided to walk. A short cut through the park took her out on to the road, and along it towards the graveyard. At the spot where Paul-Henri had died, she paused and looked down the bank, trying to imagine the scene. Then, shaking off horror, she pressed on to the walled enclosure surrounded by open fields, and went in through the wrought-iron gates.

The usual jumble of funerary adornments confronted her: marble angels, wrought-iron crucifixes, stone slabs of all shapes and sizes, artificial flowers enclosed in glass domes fogged with moisture.

She had no difficulty in picking out the family vault of the Fleurys, which was on a much grander scale than anything else. Elaborate wrought-iron railings surrounded an erection like a small chapel, with a stone urn surmounting the roof. The Fleury coat of arms adorned the entrance to the vault, and the side walls had been divided by intricate carving into panels on which the names of departed Fleurys had been inscribed. The newest-looking inscription commemorated Adrienne's husband Edouard, who had died eleven years ago to the day. Adrienne's flowers, still fresh, were on the ground in front of it. But what was it, Celia wondered, that she was not supposed to see?

Suddenly it struck her. There was no inscription commemorating Paul-Henri.

She walked right round the tomb to make sure, then searched the rest of the graveyard. Paul-Henri was not there.

Why not? He had been killed less than a kilometre away. Why had he been buried elsewhere? And why had Adrienne been so anxious to prevent her from realizing this?

Pondering various possible explanations, all of them disquieting, she turned back towards Fleury.

EIGHT

When Judge Vautrin received the dossier he had asked
for from Archives, he thrust it into a drawer without
looking into it. He did not need to, because he had a very
clear memory of the sordid story that it contained. He
had taken the file out of circulation to make sure that
Inspector Picot did not see it.

His conscience was clear. He had a duty to protect
the service from any suggestion of political prejudice.
Inspector Picot was a headstrong young man with a strong
left-wing bias, and Raynal was not much better. There
was no logical reason to suspect a connection between
the death of Miss Greenwood and the eleven-year-old
events recorded in the dossier, but if Picot saw the record
he would immediately leap to conclusions prompted by
his political views. In no time he would be in Fleury,
listening avidly to gossip from villagers and estate servants. The media would soon find out what line the investigation was taking. The service would be faced with the
old accusations of left-wing prejudice against people of
power and position, it would be the Bettencourt scandal
all over again.

But he had to be even-handed. He must also protect
the service from accusations of right-wing bias, and a news
story in several of the morning papers posed a danger on
that front which must be guarded against. So when Picot
made his routine morning call to report progress on the
case, he passed one of the papers to him across the desk.

'Inspector, what do you know about this?' he asked,
pointing out the article he had marked.

147

Picot read it. Headed 'A Mystery at Fleury', it was about a deed box which had allegedly been found in a well by members of the Fleury family. The main source was 'a landless peasant by the name of Jean Sorel', whom the papers described charitably as 'an individual with a reputation locally for eccentricity'. They recorded his claim that the box contained property which was rightfully his, and also that no one at the château had been available to comment.

'Well, Inspector?'

'Sorel came to our incident centre with the same story, Monsieur le Juge. He alleged in addition that the inhabitants of the château had murdered Greenwood to silence her, so that they could keep the box and its contents for themselves.'

'And what action did you take?'

'None, Monsieur. I saw no reason to take notice of the ramblings of a drunken peasant.'

'A grave error of judgement, Inspector.'

'With respect, Monsieur le Juge, I understood you to say that I was not to undertake any *démarche* which might be interpreted by the press as vexatious to the Fleury family.'

'This is different,' said Vautrin impatiently. 'Sorel will have repeated to the media his allegation that they murdered Mademoiselle Greenwood. They will have suppressed it to avoid actions for defamation by the family. But unless we follow up the story, we will be accused by the media of protecting privileged people and failing to investigate facts which might incriminate them.'

In other words, Picot thought, justice only prevails if it has the approval of the media.

Vautrin looked again at the news story. 'They say here that a man called Naudet confirms Sorel's story to some extent. I suggest that you question him as soon as possible.'

Picot turned to go without answering, though his expression of dumb insolence could hardly have been lost on Vautrin. Taking Raynal with him, he set out for Fleury. 'We are now facing left as well as right, Michel. We are afraid of displeasing the right-wing press by persecuting the family at the château, but we are also afraid of displeasing the left-wing press by failing to take notice of accusations which have been made against them.'

They found Naudet trailing haymaking machinery behind a tractor in one of Jean-Louis de Fleury's fields. He was a well-built man in his late twenties whose modish hair style involved a pony-tail. He confirmed the story of the accident at the well. 'When I came back from lunch André and Monsieur de Fleury had hauled the tractor away from the well with a chain and tackle and yes, there was something in the van that looked like an old tin box, which Monsieur de Fleury hid quickly under his coat.'

'How big was this box?' Picot asked. 'Show me.'

Naudet's hands enclosed a space the size of a small deed box. Sorel's vivid imagination had made it four times the size.

'According to him,' Picot went on, 'whatever was in this box was put in the well by his cousin.'

'No. He's *cinglé*, that one. His cousin couldn't have hidden anything down that well because he didn't occupy the farm till the sixties. My grandad says the well was sealed up around 1940. It went dry, he says, and they filled it up to stop children falling in.'

'Couldn't it have been opened again later and something put in?'

'I doubt it, no one knew it was there. It wasn't young Marchant's fault that the tractor fell in, the timbers covering it were overgrown with grass and weeds so you couldn't see there was a well there.'

'The Englishwoman who was killed, did you see her near the well while all this was going on?'

'No. Why should she be there?'

'Sorel says she was.'

Naudet laughed. 'That old fool's cooked in wine.'

149

'We'll have to talk to your grandfather. Where do we find him?'

'At my brother's place. La Bruère.'

As Picot and Raynal turned to go, Jean-Louis de Fleury came hurrying across the field towards them. He was furious, and his voice had risen to a falsetto screech. 'Get off my property at once. I'm not having the media putting their nose in my affairs.'

When Picot explained who they were and produced his authorization, Jean-Louis began to relax. 'Oh. That's different, you must excuse me. I suppose you've been asking young Naudet about this story that Jean Sorel's been putting round, about a box I'm alleged to have found in the well at La Roulandière. I hope you won't take his malicious fantasies too seriously, because Sorel's a hopeless drunk with a grudge against the family.'

'So there was no box in the back of your vehicle when Naudet came back from his meal?'

'There was a box, but it was not full of hidden treasure. What he saw was a tool box that I brought from the house with equipment for pulling the tractor to safety. Good day, gentlemen.'

The two detectives walked back to their car. 'Did you believe him, Jacques?' Raynal asked.

'Not entirely, and whether I did or not doesn't matter, we're supposed to follow it up. Vautrin's orders.'

Avoiding the village bar, which was full of journalists drinking in gossip from the locals, they obtained directions to La Bruère from a passing postman and tracked Naudet's grandfather down to his brother's farm, where they found the old man sitting under a vine trellis by the house. He was too feeble to work in the fields, and had surrendered the farm to his eldest son. But his mind was clear, and he remembered exactly why the well was sealed up.

'It happened in the summer of 1940,' he explained. 'The Boches were advancing and the refugees from Paris and those parts were streaming along the roads, and the Ger-

150

mans were attacking the refugees with their dive-bombers, Stukas they were called, that made a terrifying noise as they swooped to the attack. The object was to spread panic among the refugees so that they blocked the roads and made it more difficult for our troops to move into position. And one of the Stukas, no one knows why because it was miles from the road and the refugees, one of them dropped its bombs right in front of the farmhouse at La Roulandière, *poum!* like that.

'Well, Alfred Laborde, who had that land, he had gone to the army, and his wife was carrying on as best she could. The farm house had been very badly arranged by the bombs, windows gone, the roof half off, so we all helped to do what repairs we could. I was only eighteen but we all went, even the children, to make it so she could go on living there and look after the land. But one of those bombs had demolished the head of that well, and she had three little nippers so she said would we cover it over so they didn't fall in. So we did, we put two or three logs across it and planks on top, it was a useless well anyway, it had been dry for years. The Fleurys, they were good landlords then, they'd sunk an artesian borehole in the chalk after the well went dry, so that Laborde could get water all the same.

'After the war La Roulandière was let to that uncle of Jean Sorel's, and I was over there quite a lot, because one of my nieces was married to the son there, the one who died last year without a son to carry it on, and left it vacant. And none of them knew there was a disused well down the end of the yard, there was a midden over the spot as far as I remember. So if Jean Sorel says his cousin put something down the well for him to inherit, he's lost in the clouds.'

'Alcoholic clouds,' commented Picot.

'Well, he likes his little drop,' said the old man indulgently.

'And you've no idea when this box, if there was a box, got put into the well?'

151

'No, because in forty-one I was sent to Germany to do forced labour, a nasty farm it was, in Prussia, awful heavy soil and not enough to eat.' He gave Picot a sidelong look. 'They say there was some *louche* business going on at La Roulandière after Laborde came back from the army, something to do with the *résistance*, but I never got to know the ins and outs of it, so I don't want to tell you wrong.'

'Is there anyone who knows and could tell us?'

'The people who really know are dead.' He pondered. 'Go and see old Nicolas Fléchet, over at Les Bardins. He might remember something.'

Les Bardins, lost at the end of a dirt track through the fields, was a farm that looked as if the tenant had given up the struggle against too heavy odds. Fléchet was bed-ridden in the living-room of a cottage whose smell of sour vegetables and poverty reminded Picot of his own youth in the Sologne. His speech was slow and gravelly, but what he said made sense.

'Laborde came back from the army end of forty, that was when it was, and managed to do his ploughing before the bad weather set in. The château was empty by then. The old gentleman was away at some job abroad, he was in the diplomacy, and young Edouard, he was in London with General de Gaulle. Then, start of forty-one it must have been, the château was requisitioned by the dory-phores. You know what a doryphore is? A beetle that destroys potato crops, they come from America, from Colorado. We called the German army of occupation doryphores because they ate up everything.

'Well, they set up some kind of headquarters in the château and they were soon confiscating all the produce they could find from all the farms round about including of course La Roulandière. We all had to cheat a bit or we'd have starved, but it was difficult, they sent inspectors round to look for pigs hidden in back bedrooms, that sort of thing, and if they found one, *hop*! You were off to forced labour in Germany.

152

'At that time, quite early in the war, the doryphores were only occupying half of France, the North. The southern half was supposed to be presided over by poor old Marshal Pétain, though of course he had to keep in line. The border between the two was only thirty kilometres south of us, and there were border guards who checked everyone's papers when they crossed. If you were a Jew, it was safer to be in the non-occupied zone, but if you tried to cross into it with false papers that weren't good enough, *hop*! you were under arrest and off to the gas chambers.

'Presently a whisper went round that Laborde was working for the *Maquis*. Some believed it, but some said he'd put it around himself. They claimed he'd got too close to the doryphores in the château, telling them about the pigs in his neighbours' back bedrooms so they wouldn't look too hard at the one in his own. They thought he'd pretended to be in the *résistance* so he wouldn't smell so much like a collaborator. But I think they did him an injustice. It was never proved that he'd informed on anyone, and what he was doing, so people who'd helped him said, was smuggling Jews across the border at night into the unoccupied zone, at a place where it wasn't heavily guarded. He'd pick them up in Beaugency on market days, someone in the network there would pass them on to him, and he'd bring them to La Roulandière in a covered cart he had, and hide them in a cellar till there was a dark night when he could slip them over the border.

'That went on for some time, and then one morning early the postman found Laborde lying in a ditch by the roadside with a bullet through his head. When the neighbours went to the farm and asked his wife what had happened, she said, yes, he'd been helping Jews to escape and someone had told the Gestapo and they'd come and got him. But she was looking shifty as well as shocked, and some said she was lying, and there was a mass of black-market food in the house. Well, we all cheated a

153

bit, but what she had was beyond the bounds of decency.

'So a lot of people thought she was lying when she said it was the Gestapo took Laborde and shot him. What they argued was, if the Gestapo had caught Laborde working for the *résistance*, his wife and children would have been for it too. And presently another story was going the rounds, that he'd been shot by an execution squad from the *Maquis*, and for why? He'd been on the take. He'd get those poor miserable Youpins up near the border, then he'd say right, I'll get you across but first you're going to give me all the bits and pieces of jewellery and whatnot that you've got sewn into your clothes. And if you don't, it's the next border post for you, which means you're on your way to the gas chambers. So of course they were terrified and gave him everything they'd got hidden away to start a new life somewhere safe, and then he'd put them across the border.

'The story was that the *résistance* had found out what he was doing and that was why they'd shot him. Maybe they did, maybe they didn't, but a lot of people believed it, and I think it must have been one of them who denounced Madame Laborde to the Boches, either for the border-smuggling or just for black market, I don't know which. Anyway, she and the children were bundled on to one of the convoys for Germany, and were never heard of again.

'So if you say there was a box hidden in that well, Inspector, then I can guess what was in it.'

'Could she have got the well unsealed again, and hidden it down there when the *Maquis* got after her husband?'

'Easy, the cover was only wood and the well was dry, if it was a solid box she could just throw it down, and no one any the wiser. She'd be dead scared after her man was shot, she wouldn't want anyone to find the stuff he'd taken off the Youpins.'

He paused. 'Mind you, there was a lot of stories going around after the war about what happened in those days, people playing off old scores and saying this and that. Who knows if the one about Laborde was true?'

As the two detectives drove back to headquarters in

Orleans, Picot said: 'Sorel is a fantasist, but I don't think he and Naudet invented that box. I think it exists.'

'If so de Fleury is lying and the château's hanging on to whatever's in it.'

'Let's imagine it's stuffed with a treasure of Ali Baba proportions. Suppose Sorel's right, and Greenwood arrives on the scene while they're gloating over it. They're afraid someone will claim it if the story gets out, so they have to shut her up, don't they?'

'But Jacques, they don't need to kill her. She doesn't understand French, she's a foreigner, who's she going to report them to? They can easily spin some tale to put her off.'

'Anyway, are the Fleury finances so dried up that they want to hang on to a few miserable little gewgaws to help balance their books?'

'They could be,' said Raynal.

'Yes, Michel. In conformity with our instructions from Monsieur le Juge, we will make an inquiry into the state of their finances.'

They spent the rest of the morning trying to find out how well-heeled the de Fleurys were, though some of their conclusions had to be the result of guesswork. Madame de Fleury's pension as an ambassador's widow was probably enough to keep an old lady in comfort, but minuscule compared with the costs of running a place the size of Fleury. Gossip in business circles in Orleans suggested that the Marchant furniture warehouse was struggling to survive, and that its delays in paying its suppliers were getting longer and longer. His wife's poplar trees were a long-term investment rather than a steady source of income, and by all accounts the Marchant son's farming operations were only marginally more ambitious than Queen Marie Antoinette's dilettante proceedings in the Hamlet at Versailles. Jean-Louis de Fleury was considered locally to be an efficient farmer. But his holding was not much larger than one of the bigger peasant farms, and its profits had to be modest.

'So how do they keep that place going?' Picot

155

wondered. 'There must be a mass of investment income somewhere.'

'But which of them has it? The old lady?'

'Not enough by today's standards. It occurs to me to ask myself: what was Madame Jean-Louis de Fleury's maiden name?'

It turned out to be Bouvet. She was one of two daughters of a prosperous washing-machine manufacturer who had sold out to a big conglomerate in the seventies. His death five years later had made the two girls heiresses on a mouth-watering scale.

'She's keeping the whole place afloat,' said Raynal excitedly. 'She has the whip hand and when the others want to buy a tractor or a new dress, they have to humiliate themselves and beg her to disburse. So when they get a windfall, they're dead keen to hang on to it.'

'Precisely. And if one of them's committed a crime he's not on his own. They'll stick together because they've all got an interest in helping him to hush it up, so that Madame Jean-Louis doesn't fly off her hinges and cut off the funds.'

'When you say "all", who d'you include?'

'Jean-Louis and Emile, certainly. Among the others, I don't know. Not the old lady, and probably not the two youngsters.'

'So you think the Greenwood killing was a collaborative job?'

Picot thought about this. 'The cover-up certainly was. The villagers say Marchant has been seen riding a motorcycle, and de Fleury's the right size for the pillion passenger.'

'But Jacques, why could they have wanted to steal those wretched letters? And why on earth would either of them have wanted to murder Greenwood? Wouldn't we be better employed looking for sexual deviants in the Sologne?'

*

156

Unknown to Picot, the château had been under siege since early morning. The wrought-iron gates leading to the entrance court had been shut as usual the previous night, and this morning they had not been opened. Outside them stood a motley group of men, some with recording gear. There was even a television team.

'So the TV is interesting itself in us,' Adrienne complained, standing at a window. 'Are we really to be served up to the *téléspectateurs* as a titbit between the washing powders and the deodorants?'

An angry buzz of conversation rose from the excited knot of journalists.

'Something new must have happened,' said Celia. 'I wonder what.'

Adrienne drew her away from the window. 'Come, let us retire in case they see us. If we take no notice, perhaps they will go away.'

But before they could settle down to their morning routine they were drawn back to the window. The noise from the media had risen to an excited roar, for a reason which became clear at once. André Marchant was walking across the courtyard towards them.

He went up to the gate, and spoke to the crowd through it. Microphones were thrust through it at him. So was the TV team's camcorder.

'Oh, what is he telling that *canaille*?' asked Adrienne, distressed. 'This must be Emile's idea, he is too much a coward to confront them himself, so he sends André. But why did he not leave it alone?'

Whatever André had to say obviously excited the media to fever point. For several minutes questions were shouted at him from all sides. He answered some of them, then turned away with a dismissive wave of the hand and went back into the house.

Celia and Adrienne withdrew again from the window. 'I understand absolutely nothing of all this,' complained Adrienne. 'They can't be there because of the killing of the unfortunate but boring Greenwood?'

157

They both found it difficult to settle down with a media rabble at the gates. Celia tried in vain to concentrate on a long article in *Le Figaro*, and Adrienne sat at her writing desk with a pen in her hand, trying to write a letter.

Suddenly footsteps pounded past the windows on the garden side of the house. Celia looked up as a second figure rushed past. It was Chantal, in hot pursuit, shouting something angrily.

Presently renewed cries from Chantal began coming from the kitchen quarters. Adrienne rose from her reverie. 'Oh, what is happening now?'

She went to see, but was met in the doorway by Antoinette. 'It is Monsieur André, Madame. He is hurt, come quickly please.'

Followed by Celia, she hurried into the kitchen. André was sitting on a chair, very white, with blood pouring down his face. Chantal was standing over him in a towering rage. *'Voyou! Crétin! Traître!'* she shrieked.

'Stop that noise at once, Chantal,' commanded Adrienne.

'You wait till you hear what he's done,' she retorted.

Ignoring her, Adrienne examined her grandson. But as she bent over him, he fainted and slipped from the chair to the floor.

Adrienne took charge firmly. 'Antoinette, a blanket to put over him. Chantal, telephone at once for Doctor Pascal. Celia, the first-aid box. On the top shelf of the bathroom cupboard.'

Celia hurried upstairs. When she came back with the box, Jean-Louis was in the hall. He had wrested the telephone from Chantal and was barking orders into it.

In the kitchen, Adrienne was kneeling beside André, sponging his face. He had a black eye, and a deep cut in his chin, but most of the blood was from a long scalp wound over his ear. His eyes were open and he was trying to sit up, but Adrienne made him lie down again.

'Pascal is coming at once,' said Chantal, returning. 'I am sorry that Emile lost his temper. But really, André, you deserved a hiding. Your foolishness has betrayed us all.'

'Leave him alone,' commanded Adrienne sternly. 'If you cannot be quiet, Chantal, you must go.'

Jean-Louis came back from the telephone. 'I thought it wise to tell Pascal to come in the back way through the farm.'

'Why?' cried Adrienne. 'It will take much longer and that cut on his head should be sutured at once.'

'Because if the newshounds see a doctor arriving they will naturally want to know why. Fortunately André had the good sense to run along the terrace. If he had come by the courtyard shedding gore everywhere, we could have been faced with headlines about Emile's obscene brutality on every front page in France.'

Emile came hurrying in, still scarlet with rage. 'Call me brutal if you like, but there's a limit to what I'll put up with. André, you little *crapule*, you've bankrupted me.'

'Do be calm, Emile, relax,' said Jean-Louis. 'All is not lost by any means.'

'How can I relax when financially I'm in the shit?' Emile bellowed.

'You're not. Think, imbecile.'

'My husband is not an imbecile,' wailed Chantal.

'The imbecile is André,' yelled Emile.

Adrienne rose. 'Enough of this *tohu-bohu*. Go, all of you, and leave poor André alone. When Pascal has attended to him I shall ask him what all this means, because I understand nothing of it. And afterwards, if I think it necessary, I shall send for you.'

'Yes. Come, Emile,' said Jean-Louis. 'Perhaps I can make you see sense.'

He shepherded the Marchants out of the kitchen, with the argument still going on. Celia assumed that she too had been dismissed, and followed at a discreet distance.

Jean-Louis was still preaching sweet reason. 'Surely it is obvious to the meanest intelligence, my dear Emile,

159

that nobody but us knows what was in the box? The solution to our problem is obvious.'

Light dawned on Emile. 'Oh. Oh! You mean we hand over the rubbish to the yids and keep the valuable stuff for ourselves.'

'Ah. Enlightenment at last,' said Jean-Louis wearily.

'We're saved,' cried Emile. 'Why didn't I think of that before?'

'Because you have the brains of a sparrow,' said Jean-Louis languidly.

Chantal turned, and saw Celia standing at the far end of the hall, having evidently heard too much. Furious, she went on the attack. 'Why are you holding on here, day after day, where you are not welcome? Poor *Maman* cannot think of a way to get rid of you, but you tire her out, you make her expire from boredom.'

'That is not the impression she gives me.'

'Because she is polite. Why do you not go?'

'I shall leave when it is possible for me to do so.'

Jean-Louis seized Chantal's arm and more or less dragged her out of the house. The heavy front door banged shut behind them.

Celia returned to the salon and took up the newspaper, but was too obsessed by curiosity to concentrate on it. But she was frustrated by lack of information and could make no sense of the agitated carry-on that she had just witnessed.

After what seemed a long time Adrienne came in to look for her.

'The doctor has just left,' she reported. 'Andre's jaw is not broken as I feared, only bruised very badly. But the cut in his head needed a suture of ten stitches.'

'Horrors. Emile must have been out of his mind.'

'When he loses his temper he is like an elephant in a porcelain shop.'

'Is André very shaken?' Celia asked.

'He is anxious to explain his actions. And for some reason he wishes you to hear his explanation too.'

160

André was lying propped up on cushions on the chaise-longue in Adrienne's boudoir, with an enormous bandage round his head. His black eye had developed spectacularly, and there was plaster over the cut on his chin.

'I shall tell you the story from the beginning, *Grand-mère*,' he began.

'But do not exhaust yourself with too much talking,' Adrienne urged.

'I'm OK, *Grand-mère*, let me explain what happened. While Naudet was away having his lunch we hauled the tractor away from the hole with the tackle that Uncle had brought in his van, and I spotted this tin box at the bottom of the well. So I used the rope to climb down and get it out. It wouldn't open, but it rattled as if there was metal inside, so we decided to put it in the van and take it home where we could use tools to force the lock. Just then Naudet came back, and Uncle put his coat over the box to hide it. He didn't offer Naudet a lift back to the farm either, so on the way back I asked him why, and he said we weren't telling anyone about the box, in case there was something valuable in it that we'd want to keep for ourselves.

'So we opened the box in his study and he was quite right, it was almost full of brooches and rings and gold coins and one or two quite big things, a diamond necklace and so on, all very dirty but obviously valuable. And Uncle said again that if the news got out every family that had farmed La Roulandière would say it was theirs. Besides, strange things had happened under the Occupation and people connected with the *Maquis* would make up stories to stake a claim. And he said particularly not to tell Anne-Marie, because she had very exaggerated ideas of right and wrong, and would probably be awkward and say we must try to find the owners.'

'That's true, bless her,' said Adrienne. 'From where did she inherit a conscience? Not from either of her parents.'

'I'm a bit disgusted with myself for having gone along with Uncle's line,' said André. 'But I thought, if we had some money I could study law instead of struggling with that wretched farm. So I said of course I would tell Papa about the find, but Uncle said no, he would tell him himself. And that evening when Papa came home from work he did, and the most awful row broke out. Apparently Uncle Jean-Louis told him that the money from selling all that stuff was needed to put the estate on a sound basis. And when Papa said that his business needed more investment urgently, Uncle said the business was on the rocks and not worth investing more money in, and anyway the box was in Uncle's safe and that was where it was going to stay.

'So when Anne-Marie asked me what the row was about I didn't tell her. I felt bad about that, because whenever our parents do something horrid we always tell each other. But I still thought I might not have to farm, because the box was found on land belonging to our side of the family, and Uncle would have to give him some of the money at least. I was right about that, because in the end they made it up and agreed to go half in half.

'Then last night Naudet and I went to the Hôtel du Commerce for a drink after work, and he told me what the old men were saying, the ones who remembered the Occupation, and it was a nasty story. According to them a man called Laborde had taken all that stuff off Jews he was supposed to be escorting to safety. So I thought, Oh God, everyone in France feels bad about what happened to Jews under the Occupation, even if they won't admit it. The idea of clinging on to that dirty creature's ill-gotten gains really made my stomach heave.

'Last night in bed I thought about it a lot. And in the morning when I saw the journalists waiting outside the gate, I thought I'd better go and tell them we'd found the box, and intended to hand over the contents to a Jewish charity. But I decided not to warn Papa first, because it would only lead to a lot of argument. Actually, the journalists seemed to know most of the story already.

'When I went back to the house Papa asked me what

I'd been saying, so of course I had to tell him. I knew he'd be angry, but I didn't expect him to use me as a solid block on which to smash one of the dining-room chairs.'

'They weren't real Louis Quinze,' said Adrienne. 'Only Second Empire imitations.'

He turned to Celia. 'I've told you all this because I want you to go to Anne-Marie and ask her to forgive me for not confiding in her. I knew she'd got a real sense of right and wrong, she'd have said at once that we must try to identify the owners. I disgust myself for not following that line from the start. Talk to her, please, and bring her back here.'

'Yes, my dear Celia, please go,' Adrienne begged. 'I long to have our little Anne-Marie back at home.'

As Celia drove to the Château de Premay, she tried to make sense of André's revelations.

She had been right in assuming that there had been a windfall of doubtful legality, but wrong in thinking that it had fallen in Emile's direction. It was Jean-Louis who had found the box and put the contents in his safe. He had not intended at first to share them with Emile, because he saw no point in pouring money into a semi-bankrupt business. But he had been forced to change his mind. Why?

Nothing fitted. According to Antoinette, it was Emile who had pursued Jane into the Sologne in Adrienne's car. That made him the murderer and Jean-Louis the accomplice. But it was Jean-Louis who had found it necessary to buy Emile's co-operation by offering him a share in the windfall. Emile must be the accomplice, not the murderer. Something was the wrong way round.

But suppose Antoinette had been lying. It was possible, thinking back. There had been something oddly defensive and devious in her manner as she accused Emile. She was devoted to Philippe. She had panicked when she thought he was under suspicion, and nothing Celia could say had calmed her. Had she tried to protect her ewe-lamb from suspicion by diverting attention to another possible suspect? There were only two to choose from. If she still hoped that Jean-Louis would recognize Philippe, she could not afford to harm or offend him. So she had picked on Emile.

Suddenly, Celia's confidence ebbed away. This whole theory was a mare's nest. Jane had been killed by a stray rapist, there were plenty of them about. The letters had been stolen in Orleans by a pair of casual muggers. The whole elaborate structure of suspicions and suppositions collapsed like a house of cards.

No, she decided, taking a grip on herself. There was one solid fact to go on. She had not imagined that revealing moment under the carport in the courtyard. And she realized now that she had actually seen Emile's share of the windfall being handed over, that was what Jean-Louis had been hiding inside his jacket. The incident in the parking bay was the starting point of the chain of reasoning. It all hung together, there were no flaws in her logic. But she was faced with her usual trouble. There was not a vestige of proof. The thought of pouring out all this conjecture into Inspector Picot's sceptical ear made her cringe.

Anne-Marie was playing tennis when Celia arrived. She was delighted when Celia explained what all the mystery had been about and deeply moved by André's change of heart. On learning that André had been hurt, she was anxious to start back to Fleury at once.

On the way Celia broached a delicate subject. 'Anne-Marie, I want to ask you about something that seems to be a family secret. Why isn't your uncle Paul-Henri buried in the family vault?'

'Oh. You don't know?'

'No. It seems odd, when he died in a traffic accident just outside the village. Your grandmother showed me the place.'

'I know, she does that to everyone. I think she's made herself believe it, but it's not true. This is something we don't talk about much, and I really shouldn't tell you. It wasn't an accident, he killed himself.'

'Anne-Marie, are you sure?'

'Yes. Archi-sure. I think he must have done something dreadful. He couldn't be buried there because the Church said he'd died in mortal sin.'

'Horrors, Anne-Marie, how dreadful.'

'I know. I was pushed off to the Languedoc cousins when it happened, to keep me from knowing about it. I only found out when I was fourteen or so, because we all went to the cemetery on the Day of the Dead, and I suddenly saw that Uncle Paul-Henri wasn't commemorated in the inscriptions on the Fleury vault. When I asked why, *Grand-mère* had a sort of seizure and Papa took me aside and told me he'd killed himself and that was why. And I was never to talk about it to anyone, least of all *Grand-mère*, because she'd adored Paul-Henri and couldn't bear to hear the thing mentioned.'

'But why did he kill himself?'

'I've no idea, but whatever happened must have been pretty horrific to get *Grand-mère* into such a state.'

'But you've no idea what did happen?'

'No, I didn't like to ask. Philippe started dropping some heavy hints about it when he was attacking the family in that bar, implying that it was very nasty indeed, but I choked him off.'

'There's something here I don't understand at all,' said Celia. 'If Paul-Henri's botanical book is published, won't it revive this awful scandal that your grandmother wants forgotten?'

Anne-Marie frowned. 'No, that's been taken care of. You see, *Grand-mère* had half persuaded herself that the horror, whatever it was, didn't happen, and she was determined to arrange a proper memorial of Uncle Paul-Henri. Papa and Aunt Chantal were very much against it because they saw it would revive the scandal, but she refused to give up the idea. In the end they had to let the project go ahead, but on condition that the book was not published with his name on it, but under a *nom-de-plume*.'

Enlightenment dawned. 'And is that why someone who wasn't French had to edit it?'

'Of course. Everyone in French botanical circles would remember what happened all those years ago. If it was edited by one of them, he would have to know that the materials came from Fleury, and that Paul-Henri was the real author. The secret would be revealed, and the family would be surrounded once more by scandal. So *Grand-mère* agreed. The memorial to Uncle Paul-Henri would be anonymous, but it would be better, she decided, than no memorial at all. Celia, how soon can I come and work at your nursery?'

'Any time after I get back,' said Celia, and drove on in silence with her mind in turmoil. The puzzle was beginning to arrange itself in a pattern, but an essential piece was missing. She still did not see what motive Jean-Louis and Emile could have had for wanting to steal Jane's letters. Was there really something in them that the police must not see?

Suddenly, shamingly, the answer stared her in the face. She cursed herself for a numbskull. She had assured Picot that the letters contained nothing incriminating, but she had misled him grossly.

Adrienne had discouraged Jane from taking her taxonomic queries to a member of the French botanical fraternity, for a good reason. Jane must be kept out of contact with people who might tell her things about Paul-Henri that Adrienne did not want her to hear. But Jane had defied her and consulted the Professor of Botany at Orleans University. The professor had provided her with some 'interesting information', and in her last letter to her mother she had said that she proposed to investigate it.

When summarizing the contents of the letters for Picot's benefit, Celia had considered this episode irrelevant and had almost failed to mention it. In the event she had passed over it far too lightly, and had failed to make it clear how long before Jane's death her consultation with the professor had taken place. Emile and Jean-Louis had both read her letters. The guilty one would have realized the danger at once. When the police saw

166

that the interview had occurred only two days before Jane died, they would have interviewed him as a matter of routine.

They would have discovered that the information he had given Jane had nothing to do with the classification into species and genera of France's wild flowers, and they would have wondered what she found out when she started to investigate.

NINE

It was clear to Celia that Inspector Picot had not interviewed the Professor of Botany at Orleans University. If he had, he would know enough by now to make an arrest, or at least take Jean-Louis and Emile in for questioning. It was all her fault. In mentioning the professor she had said nothing to suggest that he might be a material witness, and he had not followed up her vague hint. It was her clear duty to take corrective action and put him on the right track.

But she had always had a morbid dread of going to the police with vague theories she could not prove. It was something she avoided if it was humanly possible, and she was determined to avoid it now. She would start to collect the evidence she would need to prove her point. She would present herself to the professor as Jane Greenwood's chief mourner, anxious to know what they had discussed in the last few hours of her friend's life, and make him repeat to her whatever horror-story he had told Jane.

On the pretext of yet more consultations with the firm concerned with Jane's *pompes funèbres*, she set off into Orleans in search of him. But at the University disappointment awaited her. Georges Orbigny, the Professor of Botany, was away, attending an ecological conference in Rio de Janeiro. His secretary remembered that an English lady had visited him shortly before he left, but did not know what they had discussed. A few days ago, a policeman had called to say that the very same lady had been

168

murdered in the Sologne, and would Professor Orbigny please ring the commissariat as soon as he got back.

Frustrated, Celia refused to give up her search for evidence. At least she could find out what the great mystery was that surrounded Paul-Henri's death. The back files of local newspapers could always be relied on for that sort of information about a *cause célèbre*.

By claiming boldly to be a British freelance journalist covering the death of her compatriot Miss Greenwood, she gained admission to the morgue of the *République du Centre* where, to her surprise, the folder of press cuttings about Paul-Henri de Fleury was produced almost at once.

'You are the third journalist who has asked for them,' the clerk explained.

Celia arranged the cuttings in date order, and went through them. During the winter of 1982–3 a murdering rapist had been at work in the area round Beaugency. The press called him 'the Monster with the Van' because he always tricked or forced his victims into a van or truck, in which he raped and killed them before dumping them by the roadside. Witnesses' descriptions of the van varied, and the police suspected that more than one vehicle was involved. The cuttings described his method, which was always the same: strangulation with a scarf of red silk, of which fibres had been found under several of the victims' fingernails.

In April 1983 the killings suddenly stopped. All concerned assumed that the culprit had moved away to another area, or managed to control his murderous impulses or died. But on 14th July 1983 the evidence suggested that they were wrong.

TRAGIC END TO THE CELEBRATIONS AT FLEURY

The Monster with the Van strikes again

The celebrations at Fleury-la-Forêt of Tuesday's Fête Nationale were darkened by a brutal murder, apparently the work of the so-called 'Monster with the Van'.

The victim was Madame Jeanne Fourbin, a widow resident at the Clos des Abeilles, three kilometres from the village.

After the programme of events had closed with dancing and fireworks, Madame Fourbin could not be found by friends with whom she had arranged to take some refreshment, and it was assumed that she had changed her plans and gone home.

Early on the following morning her corpse was found by workmen, lying in a ditch by the roadside in the proximity of the village. She had been stripped, sexually assaulted and strangled, apparently with a scarf.

There is reason to fear that the sexually perverted killer who terrorized the area last winter has resumed his activity and that further murders may follow.

The rest of the story described the reactions of the workmen who had found the body, friends of the dead woman, and the authorities, who had issued warnings to women in the area to be on their guard.

There was a follow-up story two days later. Examination of the clothing found near the body showed that fibres of a red material had been caught up in the clasp of a brooch she had been wearing. The last paragraph gave one further detail.

Monsieur Jean-Louis de Fleury, son of the Comte Edouard de Fleury de Marcilly and resident at the château, deposed that he had spent only a short time at the celebrations. Because of anxiety about his father's serious illness he had left early to keep his mother company, and while taking a short cut home through the park he had seen a van parked by the roadside. His description of it fitted details

170

known from other sightings of the monster's van,
but he had attached no special significance to this
until after the tragic discovery on the following
day.

A later report added that the autopsy had found the
victim to be about four months pregnant.

So far there was no mention of Paul-Henri. But months
later, in mid-November, he was suddenly and horribly at
the centre of the case.

THE MONSTER WITH THE VAN IDENTIFIED

Suicide of Paul-Henri de Fleury

Early yesterday Paul-Henri, younger son of the
Comte Edouard de Fleury, was found dead, in
circumstances which made it clear that he was the
Monster with the Van. Beside him was the corpse
of his latest victim, Gabrielle Lenoir, 25 years, a
resident in Beaugency. She had been strangled with
a red silk scarf, which was still round her neck. After
adding the young woman to the long list of those
he had killed, de Fleury committed suicide,
apparently from remorse.

The two corpses were found in a barn on a remote
part of the family property, in a van with the engine
running and a pipe leading into the interior.

It is to be expected that the red scarf used to
strangle the victim will be found to match the fibres
caught under the brooch belonging to Jeanne
Fourbin, who was killed on the fourteenth of July.

The news story went on to describe Paul-Henri's slightly
eccentric life style; his use of the van as living quarters
on his botanical expeditions as well as for his murderous
pursuits: and the refusal of his family to face the press.
Apart from a few follow-up stories, the only other item

171

in the file was a long obituary of Comte Edouard, who had died six months later.

Celia was horrified. No wonder Paul-Henri's botanical works could not be published under his own name.

On the drive back to Fleury, she tried to think. The accepted version of what had happened in 1983 did not account for the violent reactions at Fleury eleven years later. To provoke them, there had to be an even more horrifying and sinister version which someone needed to hide. Jane must have been killed because she had stumbled on it and had blurted out her findings to the family.

What was it that she had found out?

In telling Jane the horrifying story of Paul-Henri's crimes, Professor Orbigny must have expressed doubts about the accepted version and voiced suspicions of a cover-up. This had prompted her to investigate, but into what?

Suddenly the answer was crystal-clear. She was working on Paul-Henri's herbarium specimens, each of which was labelled with the date and place of collection. In other words, she was in a position to follow his movements as he wandered round France in his van, botanizing, in the months before his death.

What Jane had found was an alibi.

It was one o'clock in the morning. Celia was in the library, and hard at work. The room was stifling, because she had closed the heavy wooden shutters and drawn the curtains so that no light showed from outside. In case a crack of light was visible under the door, the room was in darkness apart from one table lamp, shielded behind a rampart of books.

Surrounding her on the desk were piles of the portfolios containing Paul-Henri's herbarium specimens, his volumes of the *Flora Europaea*, the sheets of his botanical drawings, and a motoring atlas of France, which Celia had brought in from her car.

She had set herself the task of finding out from all this material whether Paul-Henri had an alibi for the fourteenth of July 1983, when he was supposed to have murdered Madame Fourbin. In theory there was no difficulty in locating him at that time, because each dried plant in his herbarium collection was labelled with the date and place where he had collected it. But of course the specimens had been filed in the portfolios in groups corresponding to their species and genera. Among the Papaveraceae, for example, *Papaver alpinum* had been collected in August 1980 on the Col d'Allos in the French Alps. Its neighbour in the portfolio, *Meconopsis cambrica*, had been found in the Massif Central a year earlier, and so on down the species to *Hypecoum procumbens*, collected near Saintes-Maries-de-la-Mer on the Mediterranean coast in 1979. Finding where Paul-Henri was on the day when he was supposed to have murdered Madame Fourbin involved hunting through the whole collection for the relevant date.

By the time she had been through almost a quarter of the sheets, it had dawned on her that there were no entries at all for the July of that year. What had happened to cause a gap in the middle of the collecting season? Curious, she began taking note of where he had been in the last fortnight of June, and the first fortnight in August. After working away at this for over an hour she had assembled the ingredients of an answer. On 25th June he had collected *Lychnis pyrenaica* near Saint Martin d'Arrossa in the Western Pyrenees, and *Saponaria orientalis* in the same area two days later. But according to the reference books, there was another saponaria found only in the Pyrenees, *S. caespitosa*. It was not in the portfolio, why had he not collected it? Admittedly it was rare, but so was *orientalis*, and he had managed to find that.

The book provided a possible explanation; *S. caespitosa* did not start flowering till July. Had Paul-Henri missed it because he had moved on from the Western Pyrenees? If so, where had he moved on to? July was still a blank,

173

but she had noted a scattering of entries for early August. They were all from the foothills behind Perpignan and the Mediterranean coast. Logic suggested that he would have spent the missing month in the Eastern Pyrenees, on his way through. But if so, why had she found no herbarium specimen to confirm this?

If Paul-Henri had been in the Pyrenees at the time, he could hardly have missed collecting the one Pyrenean endemic that everyone knew about, *Viola cornuta*. She looked for it among the Violaceae in the herbarium specimens. It was not there. On a sudden impulse, she double checked by turning up the corresponding page in the drawings. There it was among the other violas, beautifully drawn and coloured. He had illustrated it, but he had not collected it for his herbarium. Why?

She went back to the beginning and went through the orders, starting with the Ranunculaceae. *Adonis pyrenaica* was illustrated but not in the herbarium. The same applied to *Pticotrichum pyrenaicum*, *Iberis spathula*, and *Dianthus pyrenaicus*. According to the books all of these were predominantly or exclusively of Pyrenean habitat.

Working on through the orders, she found other gaps. There was no doubt about it, someone had removed the herbarium specimens covering Paul-Henri's collecting activities in July 1983. The evidence of what he had been doing was still there in his drawings, but to remove them would have involved a risk of their being missed. The Pyrenean plants had been drawn on sheets which also illustrated half a dozen other members of the same species. Someone had removed evidence that Paul-Henri had been in the Eastern Pyrenees in July 1983, and not in Fleury. There was no doubt who the someone was.

When had the tell-tale herbarium specimens been removed, and by whom? Almost certainly, after Jane's murder and by her murderer. One could imagine the course of events. Jane, delighted by her discovery and convinced that the de Fleurys would be as delighted as she was, had not waited for Adrienne's return before breaking the glad news that Paul-Henri was innocent after all.

Was someone at Fleury the rapist who had been active the previous winter, the man whom the press called the Monster with the Van? His murderous activities had stopped in April 1983. Then, after a gap, he had struck again on 14th July. Or had he? Could it have been a copycat killing, intended to pass muster as another attack by the rapist, but perpetrated by someone else with a totally different motive?

A possible motive suggested itself. The autopsy had established that Madame Fourbin was pregnant. Had she demanded money or threatened the father with exposure? If so, he could have killed her to protect his marriage or career.

Assuming that this was a copycat killing, who was the killer? Not Emile Marchant. He and Chantal were still living near Bordeaux at the time. They did not move to Fleury till Chantal inherited her share of the property after her father's death.

Jean-Louis then? The cuttings provided a pointer in his direction. Jean-Louis had claimed to have seen the killer's van near the scene on the night of July the fourteenth, and his description of it corresponded with the few known details about the monster's van which had been published in the press. No one else reported having seen it, and there would have been no van for Jean-Louis to see if he had killed Madame Fourbin himself. He must have drawn on his imagination in an attempt to fit Madame Fourbin's murder into the series of sex killings by the monster.

Had the attempt succeeded? Or had the village gossips been laying the murder at Jean-Louis' door in a mounting tide of accusation? And what about Gabrielle Lenoir, allegedly Paul-Henri's last victim? If she was in a position to threaten Jean-Louis with exposure as Madame Fourbin's murderer, he would need to kill her too. But this time an attempt to blame the monster would be even less convincing.

175

Was Jean-Louis capable of a diabolical plot against his own brother? Needing to kill Gabrielle, had he killed Paul-Henri too, and staged his 'suicide' in order to set him up as the monstrous serial killer and rapist, and deflect suspicion from himself? It seemed almost inconceivably cold blooded, but the story of Cain and Abel came to mind. Paul-Henri was clearly his mother's favourite, perhaps his father's also. The peccadillo which had fathered Philippe on Antoinette can hardly have endeared him to either parent. Was Jean-Louis jealous of his layabout younger brother, who led a carefree life botanizing while Jean-Louis sweated away on the farm? Like the serial killer, Paul-Henri's life style involved the use of a van. The temptation to let him be blamed for the whole series of killings might well have proved too strong.

Who had been present when Jane revealed that Paul-Henri had an alibi for Madame Fourbin's murder? Not Hortense or Adrienne, they were away at their spa. Not André or Anne-Marie, they were staying with friends in Paris. Jean-Louis, certainly, and perhaps the Marchants.

Next morning, he had followed Jane into the Sologne and killed her. Then, when Celia produced the letters, he had realized that unless they were suppressed the police would know where to find the corpse and the reason why Jane had been killed. He had confided in the Marchants, who probably had their suspicions already. They had agreed at once to help with the cover-up. They all three depended on Hortense's subsidies. If her husband was convicted of murder her moneybags would be shut for good. Jean-Louis, having recruited Emile to ride the motorcycle, had not only stolen the letters, he had mounted a savage attack on Celia. If he had not been interrupted, he would have battered her into such a state of misery and confusion that she would have been unable to give a coherent account of the letters' contents, and would have omitted all mention of Jane's visit to the botany professor.

But all this was conjecture. The only solid fact was Paul-Henri's alibi for the murder of Madame Fourbin. Celia began making a fair copy of her extracts from the herbarium entries for Picot's benefit. But before she could finish it, the door was suddenly flung open. A voice, Jean-Louis' angry screeching voice, said, 'There you are, I knew it!' as he lunged into the room.

Celia had already taken the only defence measure open to her, by turning off the table lamp. There was a crash as Jean-Louis collided with something in the darkness, something heavy that fell over with a metallic clang. Sounds of struggle suggested that the library ladder had fallen on top of him. With luck he would take a few moments to free himself. Meanwhile, she made a dash for the door and fled headlong down the great staircase.

The front doors were locked and very unwieldy, there was no time to open them. The French windows in the salon were the next best bet, but too obvious, Jean-Louis would go there next. Instead, she ran into the kitchen and down the spiral staircase into the huge vaulted store room in the basement below. It had an outside door underneath the arch of the front steps.

She unlocked the door and left it open, but without going out. Far better to hide in one of the dark recesses cluttered up with lumber while Jean-Louis rushed out in pursuit of her, then slip out quietly at her leisure.

Muffled cries came from upstairs as Jean-Louis searched for her. Furniture scraped across the floor above as he moved it. She was wondering whether she had time to slip out into the night when footsteps clattered down the cellar stairs. Jean-Louis, having found the french doors in the salon still shut, had remembered the basement door.

Finding it open he sped on out into the moonlight and made straight for her car, which was parked with the others in the shelter of the arcade. Presumably he expected her to be in it and about to drive away, but he had failed to realize that a woman in a thin summer dress with no pockets, who had left her handbag behind in her panic, was unlikely to have her car keys on her. It was now or never, she realized. As he disappeared among the cars in the arcade, she slipped out and round the corner of the house into the deep shadow of the garden.

A gap in the hornbeam hedge offered a way of escape into the woodland of the park. She hurried on, hoping he would not hear the rustle of fallen leaves as she ran. But the moon was full, she could be seen through the open spaces between the trees. Where to hide? Not behind conspicuous features, a fallen tree trunk, a stump over-grown with ivy; they were the first places a pursuer would search. But a hollow in the ground, with nothing to draw attention to it, was a different matter. She stumbled on it, plunged in, lay down, and found to her disgust that it was rather damp.

Silence. Then after a long interval, a rustle among the fallen leaves which came nearer and nearer. An impatient grunt of frustration. The noise of feet among the leaves passed by quite close, then died away. She lifted her head cautiously. Jean-Louis was heading out of the wood into the pasture on the far side.

But he was not the only danger. Shouts from the direction of the house showed that he had alerted others and made them join in the chase. She would have to get out of the park before she was found. Crouching low, she ran towards the edge of the wood, but in a different direction from Jean-Louis. A deep ditch with a stream at the bottom separated it from the fields beyond. She forded it, and found herself in a cornfield.

What next? To escape from Fleury along the roads would be risky, the family would be patrolling them in cars, looking out for her. To flee across country would not be much safer. The fields of corn and root crops had no hedges. It would soon be dawn, and anyone moving about in them would be visible from miles away. There was a telephone box in the village from which she could ring *police-secours*, but it would probably be watched.

178

But a telephone was the obvious solution. She skirted round the edge of the cornfield towards the road which led to the village, determined to knock someone up and ask to use the phone.

Who in the village was used to being woken to deal with night-time emergencies? A doctor. But there was no doctor in Fleury. The priest, then. With infinite precautions against being seen, she crept along the road into the deep shadow of the church, and knocked on the door of the presbytery till the *curé*'s housekeeper let her in.

On studying the newspapers next morning, Judge Vautrin made an unwelcome discovery. Rather sooner than he had expected, the media had resurrected the story of the younger Fleury son, who had committed suicide after a longish career as a sex-killer. And he had not yet completed his preparations for dealing with the questions he would be asked.

On going through the dossier, he was puzzled by a number of things. The investigation into Paul-Henri de Fleury's death had taken a curious turn. Several surprising leads had been followed up, but had not produced conclusive results. A general atmosphere of 'not proven' hung over various aspects of the case. He decided that he needed to find out more. The investigating judge had been Bartet, a sound man in his day. He was still alive, but must be approaching ninety. Would he remember anything about the case? Vautrin had made an appointment for this morning, to go and see.

He found Judge Bartet in a small villa in a quiet suburb bordering the River Loiret. Shrunken with age and crippled with arthritis, he was sitting propped up on cushions in an armchair in his book-lined study. But to Vautrin's relief he seemed to be still in possession of his faculties.

'I have a particular reason for remembering this case,' he said, 'because it was one of my most serious failures. The evidence of guilt was too weak. In those days we had no genetic fingerprinting to help us secure convictions

179

when other clues failed. Finally I found myself obliged to close the dossier without ensuring that justice was done.

'It was not, but let me tell you the story from the beginning.' He ran rapidly through the main features of the case, the series of sex murders during the previous winter, the use of a red silk scarf as a ligature, Paul-Henri's erratic life style and the fact that he spent part of the year living in a van, all of which pointed to the easy acceptance of the presumption that he was the guilty party.

'As I remember, his residence at Fleury covered the period in the winter and early spring when the main series of killings had occurred. Then during the celebrations on the fourteenth of July a young woman called . . . let me see, her name was . . .'

'Jeanne Fourbin,' Vautrin prompted.

'Thank you, yes. She was a beautiful creature, with deep auburn hair and a marvellous figure. She had been raped, and strangled with a red silk scarf, and a van had been seen in the village which was similar to the one used by the serial killer who had been at work during the winter. The assumption was that this latest murder was also his work.

'The autopsy revealed that she was pregnant. Later in the summer rumours spread round the village to the effect that she had been the mistress of Jean-Louis, the elder de Fleury brother. People were saying that he might have murdered her, using methods which imitated those of the serial killer which had been widely reported in the press, in the hope that her death would be laid to his account. Moreover, it was he who had reported seeing a van in Fleury during the celebrations, which might well have belonged to the serial killer. No one else had seen it.

'When I questioned Jean-Louis de Fleury about these allegations, he denied knowing the victim, except as a neighbour with whom he had occasional dealings over such matters as supplying her with logs from trees cut down in the park for use as firewood. If people in the village had seen him in conversation with her, it was for reasons such as these.

'We already knew that Madame Fourbin had lived in the area for less than three months, having moved there from Paris. Jean-Louis had made frequent visits to Paris for some years, but our investigation failed to establish that he had associated with her there. Meanwhile the rumour factory in the village had been hard at work producing fresh suggestions that the acquaintance between him and the dead woman was very intimate indeed. The Fleury family were regarded as ungenerous landlords, and their unpopularity may have influenced what was said. It was difficult to know how much importance to attach to these stories, but they were perhaps well founded enough to make Jean-Louis feel very uneasy.

'By October, his brother Paul-Henri was back home for the winter, slightly earlier than usual because his father had suffered a severe stroke and was hovering between life and death. And in November he was found in his van, asphyxiated. Lying beside him was yet another victim, a rather unattractive brunette.'

'Gabrielle Lenoir,' said Vautrin.

Bartet nodded. 'Again, she had been raped and strangled. The ligature, a red silk scarf, was still round her neck. All the circumstances suggested that Paul-Henri was the serial killer who had eluded all attempts to catch him for almost a year. If he had been in the area on the fourteenth of July, when Madame Fourbin was killed, no one had seen him. But a few days after his "suicide" his elder brother came to us with a story which he claimed to be revealing with great reluctance. On the day after the July Fourteenth celebrations Paul-Henri had telephoned him in an agitated state. He was in trouble, he said, and in urgent need of money, but unwilling to face his parents. Could Jean-Louis meet him at the bank in Orleans and hand over the quite large sum he needed to tide him over the crisis? Jean-Louis said he had done so, and produced bank documents showing that he had

181

indeed withdrawn the sum named. Until alerted to the truth by his brother's suicide, the significance of this episode had not occurred to him. But it now seemed possible that Paul-Henri had arrived at Fleury intending to join in the July Fourteenth celebrations, but had been overtaken by a sudden impulse to kill, and had gone away again after the crime without contacting his family in order to avoid being suspected.

'By this time we were very suspicious of Jean-Louis. Ever since the July murder the rumours in the village had grown in intensity, and now a new factor was added. The dead girl found in the van with Paul-Henri was said to be a confidante of Madame Fourbin's. There were vague stories to the effect that she had either attempted to blackmail Jean-Louis on the basis of what she had been told by her dead friend, or had threatened to denounce him to the authorities as a murderer. No one could say where these rumours originated, and no one came forward with information categorical enough for us to act.

'Our enquiries suggested that if these rumours were true, he had an overpowering motive. He had no money apart from the modest earnings from the farm, and was partly dependent even for day-to-day living expenses on the fortune of his wife, who was described locally as a resolute woman with a good business sense. It seemed to us unlikely that she would have parted willingly with sums which would have permitted him to placate an ex-mistress demanding money. It was also possible that the lady was demanding marriage and threatening to create a scandal, and one could imagine what the reaction of a rich, strong-minded wife with a good business sense might be.

'We had to consider the possibility that he had killed his mistress, carefully raping her before strangling her with a scarf so that her death would take its place in the series; that the threat of exposure had constrained him to kill again, even though the death of the blackmailer would intensify the suspicion against him; and that in an almost unbelievably cold-blooded attempt to fix the blame elsewhere, he had made it appear that his own brother was a demented sex killer.

'The autopsy on Paul-Henri did not confirm this hypothesis, but it did not exclude it. There was an almost empty bottle of whisky lying on the floor of the van, with his fingerprints on it and no one else's, and the pathologist confirmed that he must have drunk some of it. As we all know, it is not uncommon for a suicide to intoxicate himself before committing his act, and although some of the whisky had been spilt on his clothing, this could have been accounted for by his agitated state of mind. There was no evidence that it had been forcibly administered by another person to reduce him to a state of insensibility, and the autopsy revealed no other indication of possible foul play.'

'But Paul-Henri left no letter?' Vautrin asked.

'No. But that was not conclusive. One could imagine that a man driven to despair by the latest manifestation of his atrocious guilt would allow the gruesome facts to speak for themselves. On the other hand the scarf used to strangle the woman lying beside him did not prove him the killer. It corresponded with the fibres found at the scene of the July killing, caught on Madame Fourbin's brooch. But Jean-Louis could have wielded it on both occasions.

'In view of all these circumstances, we did not believe Jean-Louis' allegation, which no one else could confirm, that his brother had been in the district on the fourteenth of July. I made strenuous efforts to disprove it by establishing Paul-Henri's movements around that time. I pressed Jean-Louis hard to produce any diary or other record of botanical field work that Paul-Henri might have kept. All he produced was a set of beautifully executed botanical drawings of plants, with no dates or places of collection attached.

'If any diary or other record existed, we did not get to see it, because of an unfortunate coincidence. The father of the family, Edouard de Fleury, was seriously ill, and

183

might die at any moment. It was impossible to trouble a distinguished former ambassador of France on his death-bed with distressing questions based on suspicion and rumour, and the same applied to Madame de Fleury, who was in constant attendance on him. So our only informant about these matters was Jean-Louis, who was also our suspect.

'Needless to say, we did what we could to establish Jean-Louis' own whereabouts at the time of the murder. He had left the celebrations in the village quite early, but we could not discover when he had arrived home. His wife could not help us because she did not know. Jean-Louis had not joined her in their wing of the building, but had gone straight to his father's bedside in the main block. His mother was too distressed by her husband's condition to give coherent answers, and there were no servants living in the house.

'I would have liked to search the château in the hope of finding something more, but was frustrated by the kind of high-level pressure and interference that we all suffer from occasionally. I was reminded that a man whose distinguished service to his country had begun as an aide to General de Gaulle in wartime London was entitled to a certain consideration on his deathbed. Moreover the stricken household was already mourning the death of a son in horrifying circumstances. It was out of the question for me to invade it with a team of searchers and conduct a *perquisition*. Besides, what did I expect to find? If my suspicions against Jean-Louis were correct, he would have destroyed or removed the evidence. Anyway, higher authority insisted that he was not guilty; I was told that I had built up a fantastic theory on the basis of malicious gossip in a village where the family in the château was not popular.'

'According to the dossier,' said Vautrin, 'you made extensive enquiries whose purpose was not clear to me when I studied it. But I understand now.'

'You see, I was allowed to record all the enquiries I

184

had made, but forbidden to mention the reason for many of them, namely my conviction that Jean-Louis was guilty. As you will have seen, I was left without a grain of solid evidence to support my case, which would never have succeeded in court.'

Vautrin thought for a moment. 'Nevertheless you are quite certain that neither of the brothers was guilty of the serial murders committed in the winter preceding these events? And that the only people killed by Jean-Louis were Jeanne Fourbin and Gabrielle Lenoir?'

'In my own mind, yes. I was sure that Jean-Louis had taken advantage of the serial killer's activities to rid himself of the two women in copycat murders. And I was confirmed in my opinion over a year later, when a serial killer using methods very similar to our man became active in and around Angoulême. Unfortunately, he ceased his activities after six months, and was never caught.'

'So you had no evidence that the same killer was involved in both series.'

'Alas, no.'

'And without it, you had no grounds for reopening the case against Jean-Louis?'

'Precisely.' Bartet sighed. 'You will not be surprised, my dear colleague, that this affair remains absolutely clear in my mind after so many years. You will have had the same experience, it is one's failures that one remembers. One goes over the details again and again in one's mind, wondering if there is any other step one could have taken to bring the guilty person to justice.'

Driving back to the Commissariat, Vautrin decided that Bartet's suspicions were probably correct. Had history repeated itself? Had Jean-Louis de Fleury killed again to cover his tracks? Had Greenwood somehow opened up the eleven-year-old wasps' nest and put him in danger? How could she possibly have become involved? And if he was guilty, how could his guilt be proved?

185

TEN

'I shall not tell you anything, Inspector,' said Celia firmly, 'until you have informed the people concerned that Miss Greenwood's body is to be released for burial at once. When you have done so, I shall alert the funeral director, the pastor of the Reformed Church, and the grave-digger at Fleury, so that the funeral can take place at three this afternoon. When all this has been done, I will tell you who killed Miss Greenwood, and why.'

'But Madame—' Picot began.

'I shall also tell you why I am wearing a borrowed overcoat much too large for me over a filthy cotton dress in which I lay in the mud while hiding from the murderer and his accomplices; why I spent half the night in the presbytery at Fleury, being quizzed by a priest who seemed to think I wanted to confess something; why I had to persuade his housekeeper to lend me her overcoat; why you had to send a police car there to bring me here; why I shall need an armed guard when I go back to the Château de Fleury to collect my clothes and my car; and why I shall be leaving for England the moment I have extracted the corpse from your clutches and buried it.'

This recital had screwed up Picot's curiosity to the full, but one look at her flushed face showed that she was angry and determined. He rang the hospital with orders to release the body, then helped her contact the people involved in the funeral arrangements. But when she began telling her story, he realized that matters had reached a stage at which the judiciary would have to be involved, and drove her to the Palais de Justice to tell her story to Judge Vautrin.

But Vautrin was not in his office, and had not been in all morning. His clerk did not know where he was.

If someone has poisoned his breakfast coffee, Picot thought, I would be neither disappointed nor surprised.

He was strongly tempted to go to Fleury at once and take charge, but knew what Vautrin would say if he went without his authority. While they waited for him to appear, he encouraged Celia to continue her recital. When she had finished, he said: 'Madame, if you should ever lack employment, please remember that the Police Judiciaire at Orleans would be happy to make use of your talents.'

'I shall be quite satisfied if my talents get me back across the Channel intact and out of the way of that lunatic family at Fleury.'

After what seemed a long time Vautrin arrived and saw Picot waiting outside his office. 'Ah, Inspector. I was about to send for you to discuss an important development.'

When Picot drew Celia to his attention, he was startled, and eyed her dishevelled appearance with distaste. 'But who is this?'

'Madame Grant has important testimony, Monsieur le Juge, which you should hear at once.'

'Oh very well. And afterwards I will tell you my news.'

Celia repeated the tale of her exploits in condensed form. But Vautrin was far from pleased to find that his brilliant analysis of the case, with which he had intended to dazzle Picot, had been anticipated by a middle-aged amateur five feet tall, wearing an overcoat which was much too large for her.

'Inspector, why did we not interview this Professor Orbigny days ago?' he demanded. 'If we knew what he had told Miss Greenwood, we could have brought the case to a conclusion at once, instead of plunging this unfortunate lady into such confusion and difficulty.'

'Naturally I attempted to interview the professor,' said

187

Picot in near-mutinous tones, 'but like Madame Grant, I found that he had already left for South America. And with respect, Monsieur le Juge, I think I should lose no more time in returning to Fleury. There is evidence there which may be destroyed unless we hurry.'

'Oh? What evidence, Inspector?'

'The herbarium specimens from which Madame Grant drew her conclusions,' said Picot, as if speaking to a deaf child.

'That is of no evidential value, Inspector. The defence will argue that de Fleury collected no specimens during July 1983, and therefore has no alibi for the murder of Miss Greenwood.'

Picot cursed himself. For once the old fool was right.

'We will question the family, of course,' Vautrin told him.

'I am to bring them in? You wish to proceed by *procès-verbal*?'

Vautrin considered. 'No. It would provoke too much outcry in the right-wing press. You will go to Fleury and question the household yourself under a *Commission Rogatoire*.'

So that the right-wing outcry falls on me, not him, Picot thought.

He drove to Fleury, taking Raynal and Celia with him. At the gendarmerie post in the village he collected four large uniformed men, to marshal the household for interrogation and ensure that Celia was not molested while she was there.

On her way up to her room, she met Adrienne coming laboriously down the stairs. Celia felt immensely sorry for her. She was about to go through another harrowing crisis, worse perhaps than the one after Paul-Henri's death. The anxieties of the last few hours had aged her, but her face lit up when she saw Celia. 'Ah, you're back, my dear. What's been happening? The police want us all to gather in the salon, I don't understand.'

'I think it will be best if I leave it to the police to explain. Is Anne-Marie down there?'

188

'I suppose so. What was all that commotion in the night?'

'Adrienne, I'm afraid you must prepare yourself for bad news. Try to keep Anne-Marie with you, she will give you support.'

Depressed and embarrassed, Celia went on up to her room, where she washed, changed into cleaner clothes more suitable for attending a funeral, and transferred her effects to her car so that she would be able to leave immediately after it. On thinking it over, she decided to load up Jane's possessions too, to take back to her mother. When her preparations were complete, she withdrew to the comparative safety of the Hôtel du Commerce, where she intended to remain till it was time to attend Jane's funeral.

The gendarmes had herded everyone into Adrienne's salon. But before the interrogations could begin, Picot was subjected to an indignant babble of protest. To what cause must they attribute this infamous procedure? Presumably it had been provoked by Madame Grant, a tiresomely neurotic guest whose idiotic behaviour during the night had robbed them all of sleep. On hearing a noise during the night, Jean-Louis de Fleury had assumed that a burglar had broken in. On going to investigate he had found only Madame Grant, who had rushed out of the house as if her life was in danger, and had defied their united efforts to reassure and recall her.

Ignoring this outcry Picot summoned Jean-Louis into the library and confronted him with the folders of Paul-Henri's herbarium collection (though the notes Celia had made had vanished without trace). Had not Jane Greenwood communicated to him her discovery that his brother had been in the Pyrenees on July the fourteenth 1983, when he was supposed to have committed a murder at Fleury? Raising his eyebrows slightly, Jean-Louis said that Miss Greenwood had communicated nothing to him; but if it was true that his unfortunate brother was not guilty of one of the crimes attributed to him, he was glad to hear it. Picot returned to the charge. Had Jean-Louis not removed the evidence of Paul-Henri's innocence from the herbarium collection? Certainly not, that was an absurd suggestion. He was totally ignorant of botany, and would not have known which specimens to remove.

What had he been doing on the Sunday of Jane Greenwood's murder? He needed to think about this, he said. Had he attended mass? he wondered. At this distance in time, it was hard to remember.

'If you did, others will have seen you there,' Picot observed drily.

'No, I remember now. My wife and my mother were away from home, and in their absence I was less assiduous in my religious duties than usual. I spent the morning cutting up a fallen tree in the park, I can show you the place if you like.'

'Did anyone see you there?'

'I don't think so, but a lot of people would have heard the chain saw.'

'No doubt, we will be able to check that. You lunched at home?'

'Yes, that is to say with my sister and brother-in-law, who had kindly invited me because of my wife's absence.'

'And you did not at any time drive away in Madame de Fleury's white Renault?'

'I don't think so.'

'You're not sure about that?'

Jean-Louis slapped his forehead. 'Of course, I had forgotten. There was very little petrol in my car, so I took the Renault to run an errand.'

'What sort of an errand?'

'My sister suddenly remembered that she had no dessert ready, so I drove into Beaugency to get something from the pâtisserie.'

'And in the afternoon?'

'Let me see. That was the day when my brother-in-law and I went fishing for crayfish in the stream that forms the boundary between my farm and La Roulandière, and my sister came with us.'

'You had good luck with your fishing?'

'Yes. The crayfish were delicious. My sister cooked some for my brother-in-law and me, and we gave some to Antoinette Dupont for her and her son.'

'Did anyone other than members of the family see you while you were engaged in this excursion?'

Jean-Louis hesitated. 'It's hard to say. I didn't notice anyone.'

'I turn now to another occasion. On Thursday last, the day after Madame Grant arrived at the château, did you by any chance visit Orleans?'

'Yes. My brother-in-law and I spent part of the morning there at my brother-in-law's furniture factory. We needed new garden furniture for the terrace, and he offered to show me some.'

'And you arrived there when?'

'At about half-past ten, I think. May I ask why this interests you?'

'I am curious to know what method of transport you used to travel to Orleans.'

'We went in my brother-in-law's car.'

'You are sure you and your brother-in-law arrived by car and not on a motorcycle?'

'Oh really, this is too absurd. I do not possess a motorcycle, nor does he.'

'But Philippe Dupont does.'

'True, but I do not know how to ride one.'

'But your brother-in-law does, and being a pillion passenger requires no special skill.'

'Inspector, these questions bewilder me, I really must insist on knowing what their purpose is.'

'Their object will become apparent in due course, Monsieur. Please remain in readiness, in case we have further questions for you.'

'Certainly. And perhaps at some stage you will have the kindness to tell me what all this is about.'

Picot tackled Emile Marchant next. Yes, he said, he had been at home on the day of Miss Greenwood's death.

191

Jean-Louis had told him of his plan to cut up the fallen tree for firewood, and later in the morning he had heard the chain-saw at work in the wood. In the afternoon he had joined in the fishing expedition for crayfish.

In answer to further questions, he confirmed that he had indeed driven Jean-Louis into Orleans on the Thursday morning and shown him a new line in garden furniture in which Jean-Louis had expressed an interest. They had gone in his car, and emphatically not on a motorcycle.

'But according to people in the village, you have been seen riding one which they think was Dupont's. You have borrowed it on occasion?'

'Yes. I used to take part in motocross events, but the wife thought it was too risky, so I gave it up. It was Philippe's twenty-first birthday just then, so I made him a present of my machine. But I still enjoy a spin when my wife's back's turned, and he can hardly refuse when I ask to borrow it.'

Picot decided to let him go for the present and he withdrew, protesting that he had no idea 'what this nonsense of yours is in aid of'.

It was to be expected that Marchant would have co-ordinated his story with his brother-in-law's. But Picot had greater hopes of finding inconsistencies in the Dupont family's version of events. These were not fulfilled. Philippe Dupont too claimed to have heard the chain saw on the Sunday. It had started while he was still doing his muscle-building exercises in his bedroom, and had gone on all morning. After lunch with his mother in their quarters above the stables, he had spent the afternoon competing in a muscle-man competition in Paris. He and his mother had eaten their crayfish for lunch the next day, and they had indeed been delicious.

In answer to Picot's next question, Philippe confirmed that he owned a motorcycle.

'Did you ever lend it to Monsieur Marchant?'

He hesitated. 'I have done so, once or twice. It was a present from him on my twenty-first birthday.'

'And did you lend it to him on the morning of last Thursday?'

Philippe made a show of thinking about this. 'No, Monsieur. I was cutting the hedges that day, and the electric hedge-cutter developed a fault. I rode into Beaugency to get it repaired.'

'Dupont, you are not telling the truth,' said Picot, severely. 'You are lying to protect Monsieur de Fleury, because you hope that he will recognize you officially as his son.'

'He has always denied being my father,' shouted Philippe in what looked like a genuine bout of fury. 'I have no reason to protect him, my only concern is to tell the truth.'

Picot dismissed him and sent for his mother. While they were waiting for her to appear, Raynal said: 'I suspect that de Fleury has bought him by promising to acknowledge him.'

'If so, he will have bought the mother also. We shall see.'

Antoinette arrived with her mouth set in a grim line.

'The other day, Madame,' said Picot, 'you told me that Monsieur Emile had driven away early on that Sunday in his mother's Renault, shortly after Mademoiselle Greenwood left for the Sologne; and that he did not return till evening.' Picot paused ominously. 'So when Monsieur de Fleury says that he took the same car later in the morning to drive to Beaugency, he must be lying.'

'No, Monsieur.'

'No?'

'It is I who did not tell the truth. The inspector was accusing Philippe of killing the Englishwoman. I wanted him to suspect some other person, so I said that Monsieur Emile had taken Madame's car.'

'But the person who followed Mademoiselle Greenwood to the Sologne in it was in fact Monsieur de Fleury?'

'No, Monsieur. He went out in it much later, just before midday. He was away only for a short time, on some errand. He returned in time for lunch.'

193

'Is not this what Monsieur de Fleury has instructed you to say, rather than the truth?'

'No! Monsieur Jean-Louis has done me and my son a great injury, I have no reason to do him favours.'

'I put it to you that he has promised to make amends and legitimize your son, on condition that you lie to protect him.'

'No, Monsieur.'

'Madame, you admit that you have already lied once to the police. Why do you expect me to believe you now?'

Antoinette shrugged. 'I am telling the truth.'

'You are not. It was Monsieur de Fleury and not Monsieur Marchant who followed Miss Greenwood in the Renault—'

'No, Monsieur.'

'And you accused Monsieur Marchant instead because you did not wish to offend Monsieur de Fleury. You hoped, did you not, that he would change his attitude to your son.'

'No, Monsieur.'

Picot went on pressing her. But he got nowhere and ended by sending her away in disgust.

Left to themselves, he and Raynal took stock.

'They have concerted their story well,' Picot concluded. 'Even the fable of the chain saw cannot be faulted. There are always chain saws functioning on a Sunday in a wooded district like this, it will be impossible to prove that de Fleury's was silent. There will be sawdust where he says he cut up the fallen tree. No one in the pâtisseries of Beaugency will remember de Fleury's visit over a week ago at a time when they were all crowded with people buying delicacies for their Sunday lunch. If there were no crayfish in that brook on that Sunday there will be some there now, they will have seen to that. We shall discover that Marchant did indeed take de Fleury to look at furniture in his factory, but no one will have seen them arrive on a motorcycle and there will be enough vagueness about their time of arrival to permit them to have stolen the

194

letters from Madame Grant before presenting themselves there.'

'We must find a weak link, Jacques,' lamented Raynal. 'If we fail, Vautrin will mince us up to put us in a pâté.'

'I know. Let's take the young people next, a little brutality may make them give us what we need.'

But he was out of luck. They had both spent the weekend elsewhere, André in Paris and Anne-Marie with her friends the Saint-Amands, and could say nothing about what happened at Fleury on the day of the murder. Chantal Marchant also yielded nothing of interest, and insisted on telling Picot her recipe for crayfish Nantua by way of corroboration.

'There's only the old lady left,' said Picot. 'Madame Grant is obviously right in maintaining that she is innocent, and knows nothing. We must see her, but it will be painful.'

To his surprise Adrienne de Fleury entered the room in state, as if about to grant an audience to vassals, invited Picot to sit, and said she hoped their enquiries were proceeding to their satisfaction.

'Unfortunately not, Madame,' he replied.

'I am sorry to hear that, but would you please tell me why you are questioning the members of my family?'

Picot broke the news to her, trying to soften the blow as much as possible. She received it with a stony expression, and did not flinch. 'The suggestion you are making is an infamous one, it makes no sense. Why would Jean-Louis want to kill that silly, boring Greenwood?'

'To prevent her from revealing that eleven years ago he killed his brother, his mistress, and another woman.'

Was this news to her, or was she prepared for it? Her stony expression gave away nothing.

'I am sorry, I am completely bewildered,' she said. 'How could Jean-Louis have killed Miss Greenwood when he was all the time catching crayfish down at La Roulandière?'

'I have no reason to suppose that the crayfish-catching

195

expedition ever took place. It was invented completely, to provide your son with a false alibi for the time when he was murdering Mademoiselle Greenwood.'

Adrienne rose. 'Monsieur, I see no reason to prolong this very unpleasant conversation, which has become a dialogue of the deaf. My whole family is still deeply afflicted by the awful tragedy which befell us eleven years ago, why do you want to revive it? You are notorious throughout France for your prejudice against people of position in society, we all remember your hounding of Michel de Bettencourt, whom everyone knew to be innocent. But I warn you not to repeat your error. Beware of subjecting us to iniquitous procedures motivated by left-wing political motives, and surrounding us, as you did de Bettencourt, with a tumult of press speculation. We have friends who are people of influence, and we know how to defend ourselves. Good day to you, gentlemen.'

'*Mon Dieu!*' exclaimed Picot when she had withdrawn. 'A lioness defending her cub.'

'Yes. She would rather have a cub who is a murderer than no male cub at all to uphold the traditions of the family.'

'And she defends him cleverly. She threatens us with scandal, and the threat is real.'

'Unless we can make the accusation stick.'

'Michel, we have to make it stick, otherwise the media will have no mercy on us. And if that happens, we can expect no protection from Vautrin.'

The expected outcry against them was splashed all over the next morning's right-wing papers. When interviewed, Vautrin had more or less disclaimed responsibility for his subordinates' actions.

Jane Greenwood's funeral took place at three in the afternoon, in the walled graveyard just outside the village. Of all the embarrassments that Celia had undergone since her arrival at Fleury, this occasion was the worst. Being chief mourner at the obsequies of a woman she hardly knew was bad enough, without being supported in her role by Jane's murderer and his accomplices. Realizing what would be said if they were absent, the family had prevailed upon Picot to let them attend, though some of them were probably wishing they were elsewhere. They were certainly wishing Jane Greenwood was elsewhere, and not depositing herself within shouting distance of the Fleury ancestral vault, where her blood would cry out from the ground against her murderer till the end of time.

Adrienne, stony faced and upright as a ramrod, was looking straight through Jean-Louis, who stood on the other side of the coffin. She was supported on either side by Anne-Marie and André. Emile Marchant was very red in the face. Chantal looked bored and haughty. Hortense had dissociated herself from her husband and the other de Fleurys by standing apart by herself, and was making appropriate gestures of grief with a large lace handkerchief. The media crowded round, avid for sensational developments, and edged the curious knot of villagers into the background.

As there was no Protestant building available for the purpose, the Pastor of the Reformed Church summoned from Orleans had to conduct the whole of the proceedings at the graveside. Celia had managed to convince him that any attempt at hymn-singing was out of the question, but he had insisted on pronouncing a eulogy on the departed, based on biographical details for which Celia had to draw largely on her imagination.

After what seemed a long time the ceremony was over, and everyone moved out through the gate into the lane. Celia went to her car, which already contained her luggage and Jane's remaining effects, ready for her to drive away. She had already made a very full statement, and would not have to return till the case came to court.

The family crowded round her to say goodbye, and she had to let herself be kissed for the benefit of the media. Adrienne's kiss made her feel like Judas Iscariot, but Anne-Marie's hug, accompanied by a whispered 'See you soon in England, I hope', was even worse. Would she ever be allowed to see Anne-Marie again, after the abominable cuckoo's egg which she had laid at Fleury hatched out? The thought of the horrors she had left behind her haunted her throughout the long drive up the motorway to Calais.

Picot and Raynal did not attend the ceremony, for fear of over-exciting the media. They had already made their *adieux* to Celia. Picot had complimented her profusely on her part in the inquiry. Raynal was more reserved, as if he blamed her a little for landing him and Picot in the storm-centre of political scandal.

As soon as the family returned to the château, the two detectives continued their attempts to make their accusation stick. At Jean-Louis' insistence, they inspected the remains of the tree which he claimed to have been cutting down on the morning of the murder, and the trampled bank of the stream where the family hunt for crayfish was said to have taken place that afternoon. A gendarme with a fishing net failed to find any crayfish, but Jean-Louis explained that they had all been caught and eaten.

By the next morning the right-wing press was in full cry, with a replay of the Bettencourt affair on every front page. Meanwhile, the investigation was getting nowhere. Picot made ever more strenuous attempts to find out if anyone in the village had seen tell-tale comings and goings at the château, but the only result was a mass of the unsubstantiated rumours and wild allegations which were a speciality of the inhabitants of Fleury.

The pâtisserie in Beaugency could not remember whether Jean-Louis had been in the Sunday crowd of purchasers ten days ago. Enquiries at the Marchant furniture factory had failed to establish what time in the morning Emile and Jean-Louis had arrived, or what method of transport they had used. The agricultural machinery firm patronized by Philippe Dupont confirmed that he had brought in a hedge-cutter for repair on that day, but in

198

the afternoon. The lapse of time made it impossible to trace the originators of the rumours connecting Jean-Louis with the two women allegedly murdered by his brother. Intensive questioning of the Fleury family failed to reveal weaknesses in the rampart of lies which they erected around themselves.

The return from South America of Professor Orbigny brought a chink of light. Yes, he said, he and Paul-Henri had been in the same year at university, and had been friends. Miss Greenwood had indeed come to see him, and he had indeed told her that he had always been convinced that Paul-Henri de Fleury was incapable of committing the sex crimes attributed to him. On learning that Miss Greenwood was working on Paul-Henri's herbarium specimens, he had suggested that she might make a few checks. On leaving him, she had promised to do so.

Asked why he was so sure of Paul-Henri's innocence, and why he had not spoken out at the time in his defence, the professor stammered and became incoherent. Under severe questioning, he became even more deeply distressed, and the answer emerged. The two young men had become lovers on joint field expeditions, and he could not believe that a man with whom he had enjoyed a gentle homosexual relationship was capable of turning later into a rapist and mass-murderer of women. At the time of Paul-Henri's death he had been applying for various academic posts, and felt he could not afford to publicize their embarrassing love affair. Now, happily married and with children, he was even more reluctant to reveal it.

'This is our only solid piece of evidence,' said Picot gloomily. 'It will be challenged. He will be asked why he kept silent at the time of the apparent suicide. He will stammer and go red and start to cry and the defence will pulverize him.'

When Celia reappeared at Archerscroft, Bill Wilkins greeted her with a look of bewildered reproof. 'Got that

199

woman buried then, have you? The one you been on about?'

'Yes, Bill, I'm sorry it took so long.'

'Waiting around, was you, to find the murderer?'

'I don't think he'll be punished, Bill. There's not enough evidence.'

'Losing your grip, are you? You better give it up.'

'Yes, Bill, I know. I'll try to.'

'Celia, you always say that.'

It took her three days to pick up the threads again at Archerscroft, and deal with the problems that had accumulated in her absence. A supplier of organic mulch was claiming, wrongly, that his bill had not been paid. Squirrels were still getting into one of the glasshouses through the ventilation lights and breakfasting off the cyclamen corms inside. The grafts on last year's batch of tree peonies had failed, and illness among the workforce had left her short-staffed.

Only after these problems had been resolved was she able to turn her attention to old Mrs Greenwood's affairs. A phone call to Sir Hugo's solicitors established that Jane's insurance policies, plus money from the sale of the cottage, would suffice to keep the old lady in a fairly civilized residential home. Asked what should be done with the belongings of Jane Greenwood's that Celia had brought with her from France, they suggested that they should be deposited for the time being at the empty cottage, of which the neighbour still had the key.

After driving down to Sussex for this purpose, she went to the hospital, where she found old Mrs Greenwood propped up in a chair in the day room, alert but slightly lopsided about the face, and in slow but fairly secure command of her powers of speech. A long and rather tearful session of condolence followed, from which it was clear that she had been totally dependent on Jane for dealing with all the practical problems of life.

'I spoke to her on the ... day before she died. On the ... machine, dear.'

'On the telephone? She rang you?'

'No. I . . . rang her. It's expensive. She told me not to ring unless there was a . . . trouble.'

'And there was a trouble?'

'Oh yes. The . . . what d'you call it, the . . . machine had broken down.'

Gentle questioning established that this time the machine in question was the refrigerator.

'That's right, the fridge. The man came. He said it could be repaired, but . . . it would be almost as cheap to buy . . . a new one. So of course I didn't know whether to or not, so I rang her.'

Jane had ruled in favour of a new refrigerator, with the bill to be sent to her at Fleury. But Mrs Greenwood had had her stroke before the purchase could be made.

Struck by a sudden thought, Celia said: 'Did you and Jane talk about anything else?'

'Yes.' She concentrated painfully. 'She said she'd been doing some . . . what is it that policemen do?'

'Detection work?'

'That's right. She said she'd found out that . . . what was it now?'

Celia waited.

'I remember now. There was someone who was . . . supposed to have done something very dreadful, only Jane had found out that they hadn't done it. She was going to tell the people, she was sure they'd be pleased.'

Agog, Celia took pencil and paper out of her bag. 'Mrs Greenwood, this is very important, I'm going to write down what you've said. Do you remember what the dreadful thing was?'

A long pause. 'I think someone had been killed. Why is this important?'

'Because the people weren't pleased, in fact they killed Jane to stop her telling anyone else. Mrs Greenwood, I think you'll have to tell all this to a lawyer, who will write it down. And meanwhile, see if you can remember anything more about what Jane said.'

201

'Ask Mrs ... oh dear, what is her name, she lives next door to me. She was there when I phoned Jane, I ... told her all about it, she'll remember better than I can.'

Next morning she rang Picot with the news that she could provide him with two witnesses to confirm Jean-Louis de Fleury's guilt, whereupon he became incoherent with excitement and gratitude. Two days later, there arrived at the nursery an enormous array of Interflora flowers in a gilt wickerwork basket tricked out with golden yellow ribbons, with a card which read: *Avec les remerciements les plus chaleureux de Jacques Picot et de Michel Raynal.*

A week later, Anne-Marie de Fleury rang, to say that in the circumstances she would not be able to spend the summer staying with Celia and working at Archerscroft. 'I must stay with *Grand-mère* to comfort her a little, she is very unhappy.'

'I suppose she's very angry with me?' Celia asked.

'She is a bit furious, yes. But also with Inspecteur Picot, and even more with Papa.'

'And you?'

'Oh, if one's father is a murderer I suppose one might as well know. But it is very unpleasant here. Papa has been inculpated for murder, and Uncle Emile because they say he was an accomplice, but we do not know yet whether any of the others will be prosecuted for telling lies. Meanwhile they are all quarrelling about whether the château should be sold, because there will be no more money from *Maman*, who says she will divorce Papa, and Uncle Emile says his factory is bankrupt. But the worst of all is Philippe. He has invented nasty stories about how badly the family treated him and he is telling them to the newspapers and the people in the village and anyone else who will listen. *C'est pas du gâteau, tout ça!*'

'I'm sure it isn't, my poor Anne-Marie. What is to happen to you?'

'I shall be OK, because *Grand-mère* is going to take a flat in Paris. André and I are to live with her and he will study law and I shall go to university. And next year we will both spend the summer in England working at your nursery.'